Nigel Cox is the author of five novels. *Dirty Work* (1987, new edition 2006) was shortlisted for both the New Zealand Book Award and the Wattie Book of the Year, and won the Buckland Literary Award, and he was the 1991 Katherine Mansfield Memorial Fellow in Menton. *Tarzan Presley* (2004) and *Responsibility* (2005) were both runners-up in the Montana New Zealand Book Awards.

Nigel was born in 1951 in Pahiatua and grew up in Masterton and the Hutt Valley. His early working life reads like an author trying to find his way: advertising account executive, assembly line worker at Ford, deck hand, coalman, door-to-door turkey salesman, driver. Eventually, in the UK, he found his way into the book world—he worked for many years as a bookseller, with later stints at Unity Books, Wellington and Auckland, and as a freelance writer. In 1995 he became Senior Writer on the team that developed the exhibitions for Te Papa Tongarewa, New Zealand's national museum. With fellow New Zealander Ken Gorbey he led the project team that created the Jewish Museum Berlin, housed in the famous building designed by Daniel Libeskind. After the museum opened in September 2001 he joined its staff as Head of Exhibitions and Education. He returned to New Zealand in 2005, and rejoined Te Papa as Director Experience until May 2006.

Nigel was diagnosed with terminal cancer in late 2005. He continued to write, and finished *The Cowboy Dog* shortly before he died in July 2006. He is survived by his wife and their three children.

The Cowboy Dog

Nigel Cox

Victoria University Press

VICTORIA UNIVERSITY PRESS
Victoria University of Wellington
PO Box 600 Wellington

First published 2006
Reprinted 2006, 2007

National Library of New Zealand Cataloguing-in-Publication Data
Cox, Nigel, 1951-2006.
Cowboy dog / Nigel Cox.
ISBN-13: 978-0-86473-544-7
ISBN-10: 0-86473-544-8
I. Title.
NZ823.2—dc 22

Printed by Astra Print, Wellington

for Fergus Barrowman

Where the tumbleweeds roll
Beneath the sign of the cactus
And the stars shine down
On the desert road
While the mountain watches
The wind sighs its resignation
I fondle my guns
And deliver my load

Part One

Chapter One

When I was eighteen I came into my anger. It had been buried deep, along with my gunbelt, my spurs and my coiled whip. Now, equipped with a long-handled shovel I climbed the mountainside, dug, and there it was, as red-eyed as a gila monster. It got its teeth into me. I was shaken as the anger flooded through me; I knew that there was no turning back. I buckled the guns onto my hips and stood with my face to the gritty wind.

In truth it's wrong to say that they were my guns. These things matter and legally it was so, but legal is just another word for nothin' left to lose. They were my Daddy's guns and had come into my hands when he died. When he was cut down. When my Daddy was torn from this world by a coward's bullet which entered him between the shoulder blades and carried him away to the other side. He fell into my arms, and the weight of him was more than I could bear. I was only a boy then. I went to my knees and still he slipped from me, down into the red dirt and that is where he stayed. I wept over him and begged him not to leave me out here. I was twelve years old and believed that he was the one who had talked the world into existence.

I buried him there, high against the shadow of the mountain. No marker, though there was a symmetrical cactus. I didn't want him to be in any one place. He is in the whole of this place; everywhere I walk here is his body, now. This stinking mountain, this spreading, red, burned piece of dirt that goes out to where the searchin' eye cain't see no more; this land the love of which is all I have. I took not a thing from him, nothing that might have him in it. In this way I hoped I might still have him, somehow—it was a sorrowing boy's notion and went where all such notions go. His voice is gone from me and I can never remember, except suddenly, without warning, what he sounded like when he spoke. I have no creased photograph of his face. For several years afterwards I would see the backs of men's heads in the Auckland street and wait, breathing hard, for them to turn around. Sometimes I ran after such men. They all spit on me, and in time I cured myself of this habit.

I saved his guns.

I knew I could not wear them, then, so they were buried too, in another place. I grew up scrambling this mountainside and was never afraid I would forget. I took off my boots and my chaps, my bandana and my sharp spurs and buried them too, wrapped in an old coat. My hat blew away and I let it. The paint horse stood by and watched all this without expression, reins hanging. Barefoot, bareheaded, I went down the mountain and waited by the highway, so lonesome and windswept, and hung out my thumb.

And now I am back here and standing over all I survey. The anger is gone from me and as I watch the tumbleweeds roll across the floor of the valley below I could settle; I could say to the past, I will let you be, and turn and lead the horse up to the house and tie him there.

But anger never dies. It shifts, it changes shape like a restless shadow that is searching for an earthly form. You look again and it has moved. But not gone. Never gone.

And so as I go to the house I am vigilant. Tying the horse,

my eye goes to the red rim of these lands and I scan the horizon. On the highway, trucks roll like thunderheads. The wires of the pylons sway in the gritty wind. But that is how it has always been; how it should be. No riders.

I kick off my dusty boots and turn inside.

A highway vehicle collected me from the white stripe of the roadside and carried me away.

I was twelve years old, barefoot and out there alone and had to do a bit of fancy talking, which in my heart-sick state was a struggle. But the driver was kindly and anyway he had his great vehicle to ride and so I was carried away from those lands where my Daddy lay cold beneath the dirt. I felt the turning of the giant wheels on the blacktop and the roaring of the engine underneath me and I lay back in the warmth of the cab and, pretending I was tired, closed my eyes.

Through the hot afternoon we travelled north with the sun in our faces, and I squinted to make out those things which my Daddy had told me of, that lay beyond the rim of our lands. Little hamlets, each one more straggled out than the last, and hamlet people standing open-mouthed beside the roadstead, as though seeing a chariot of fire, instead of the long truck which, on that highway, are as common as jackrabbits. Mean acres of land, all fenced about and fussed over, and shanties which sell comestibles. The driver saw me eyeing these and said, 'Hongry? There's bread in there,' and passed a brown paper sack which contained sandwiches wrapped in newspaper. The drivers of the great highway are of the most human kind, full of understanding and sadness. If ever I was to leave these lands it would be to the great highway that I would go, to ride the mighty vehicles and chase the bunny rabbit's tail of the broken white line.

We came to a place where tracks of iron crossed the black of the highway and, knowing these for what they were, I asked to be set down. 'In Huntly?' said the driver. 'No one ever stops in Huntly unless they threw a rod.' But he pulled to the side.

I came around to his door to thank him. Looking down from his high window, he raised his shades. His eyes were the blue of a summit lake, nestled among broken rock. He passed down the paper sack with the rest of the sandwiches. After a moment he said, 'Get some shoes, kid. They like you to have shoes.' Then his great engine roared and he pulled away, leaving me there by the side of the road with my hair all tugged this way and that by the after-draught.

He was the last good man I saw for many a day.

My Daddy had talked of the strangeness of the lands where I now found myself and I was filled by a desire to wander and gaze. But I was not born a fool and so I moved off, slowly, like a cow that is heading peaceably to pasture, ensuring that nobody would mind me. Not that anybody was minding me except that if I loitered there I knew that somebody would.

The tracks of iron were bedded deep in the black river of the great highway and I followed them, away from the trucks and the shanties and into a little place that I knew to be a siding: my Daddy told me about that. Here, wagons of iron were standing, cold, and I walked close beside them, smelling them, which was a rich smell of rust and grease, and placed my hands on their flanks, so pitted and scratched. Weeds grew beneath their iron wheels, they stood as still as rocks and I knew these wagons had been abandoned here and would never move short of a dynamite blast, and so I walked on from them. But they had filled me with wonder.

14

Now I saw that, ahead, there were men and I became cautious. Three of them, standing in a triangle, and from the irritation in their voices I knew they were dissatisfied with their lives in the town named Huntly and would welcome the diversion of a shoeless boy to chase. So I hid, and waited, and when their backs were turned, slipped across lines of iron track, behind wagons, behind a broken building, and thus to the boundary fence, which swiftly I climbed. Beyond were fields and I soon had my feet in soft grass, which cheered me. There were bushes, and in the bushes I hid, until darkness began to fall.

I had seen how there were rails of iron which lay close within the fence and once the darkness was complete I moved along the wires. The town fell behind me and soon I was alone in the night. Above, the stars were the same stars I had seen on the mountain. Daddy and I had laid on our backs while he named them for me. He knew everything, my Daddy.

I climbed the fence and began to walk between the rails of iron. The sleepers were far apart, I had to stretch to reach each one. But the gravel between them was hard on my feet. Ahead, the rails shone faintly in the starlight and, walking between them, I felt guided, as though, ahead, there was a place where the splintered parts of me would come to a point. I strode on, powered by the sandwiches in my stomach, and, working harder, began to make my way around a long, slow curve that carried the tracks up a slope. Then I heard a sound.

From the mountainside it was possible to see trains passing in the distance and it was this that had led my Daddy to spend so much time explaining the railroad to me. But now the earth began to shake and I discovered that to have seen a locomotive from a mountainside was different from being in the living presence of one. Swiftly, I leapt from the tracks. Around the curve the great engine came. Its searchlight swung before it and found me, standing open-mouthed—immediately an air horn spoke from within the engine, an immense spear of sound which shafted through my head, making it ring. Then the machine was passing close before my eyes, a rushing wall of metal, and I was afraid. The mountain had always been the biggest thing. The fire inside it had always been the greatest power. Now I understood how the world might have dire forces which would bear down on a boy and shake his bones. That things comfortable and fascinating to be told of on a starlit night might prove overwhelming when they were rushing at your face.

At my ankles, sparks flew. I sensed down there the crushing fall of the iron wheels on the rails. A smell of burning oil and singed air engulfed me like a foul breath. But it was the passing of the wall of the train which was most impressive. My eyes flickered. Slowly, I put out a hand. I knew that it would not be wise to touch this thing but I could not help myself. The rushing wall of metal smacked my knuckles aside. I staggered and nearly fell.

In a kind of swoon, I swayed beside the track, overwhelmed, and thus was delayed in grasping that, labouring up the incline, the train was slowing. The engine had given way to wagons. Now I stepped back and saw that behind the wagons there were flatcars. And behind the flatcars: boxcars.

How like little houses those boxcars were, oblong in the night.

I remembered what my Daddy had told me, that you studied the first car to see what part of its flank might be gripped. Then you looked to see how you might progress from there along the side of the car to somewhere you could comfortably stand. A boxcar with an opening in the side was what you looked for. And now I saw one. I began to run

16

alongside the train. The trackside gravel was cruelly pointed and cut my feet. But in truth I flew. The idea of being able to become one with this rushing monster was so exciting that all pain, all reason were suspended. I saw that preceding the opening in the side of each boxcar was a ladder and that if I once grasped the ladder I would be able to hold to it while I established my position. I fixed my eye on the ladder of the second-to-last car and increased my speed. At the last moment I was suddenly assailed by a knowledge of the slicing power of the iron wheels which fell like hammers on the long anvil below. If I went down I would be cut in half. This knowledge was a weight I had to carry as I jumped. But I was raised in the physical world and from an early age could leap onto a running horse. My fingers seized the ladder. And while it was true that the knuckles of my left hand were bleeding and weakened, still I had strength enough to hold on. My feet swung in a circle in the air but my arms pulled me and soon I was standing upright, pressed against the wall of the train and plunging through the night. How it vibrated! Now, from the engine, far ahead, a second bellow came from the air horn, as though the beast resented the burden. But now it was a sound in the distance, a lonesome wail which did no more than remind you that one day you would die.

How proud I was, hanging there on the shuddering side of the boxcar, and how full of optimism. The night rushed into my face and I glanced down and was thrilled by the sight of the miles that were passing swiftly, effortlessly, beneath my shoeless feet. Along to my right there was a projecting flange and I thought it would bear my weight. I stretched a toe towards it. I saw how, if I had purchase there, I could swing out and along on one arm and thus gain the entrance to the interior of the boxcar. There, I would be able to sit in comfort and gaze out at the splendour of the passing night. This plan meant trusting myself to the strength of my bleeding left hand, but the night air was becoming cold and I felt that if I stayed where I was I would eventually loose all feeling and fall. I had to do it. But I am confident of my physical abilities and so again I launched myself. My toe found the flange, cold metal, and my good hand swung round and grasped the side of the opening. For a moment I was stretched there on the side of the train. Then, holding firmly with my right hand, I brought my trailing leg from the ladder and onto the flange. This was a precarious situation and I did not linger in it, but pressed on to the doorway.

Below the wheels clattered and, as I teetered in the opening, my thoughts were full of triumph at avoiding them. Thus I did not see the booted foot which came out of the interior darkness to hit me square in the chest and send me sprawling on the sharp gravel below.

Chapter Two

As I stand in the gritty wind of the mountainside and remember these insults to my boyhood self, I am instantly returned to that anger which once moved inside me like a river of poison. I set that anger against the wrongs that I have done—the evil that caused my anger, and the wrongs—and I stand in the face of the wind and say to myself that a balance has now been made between these two accounts and that a just order is settled upon the world.

Meantime my eyes are scanning the horizon for riders and I know that it ain't so.

My back was near broken by the fall, my head was cracked. But the iron wheels spared me and soon I was up on my feet. Within two hours there was another train and this time there was no foot to come out of the darkness. I sat in the doorway of a boxcar which had no occupants save biting flies and was carried without further incident through the night until the train came to rest in the railyards of the northern city that its inhabitants call Auckland.

They call it that instead of saying its true name, which is a word for a hole where life runs into the ground.

The dawn light upon the railyards was grey, as though it was full of airborne particles. I saw that one quarter of the sky was lighter and I headed that way, coughing—trying to silence the coughs so as to remain invisible. I crossed a road, passed down between tight-pressed buildings, and came then to a rough piece of land, with rocks. And beyond the rocks: the ocean. Of course my Daddy had painted the ocean for me with a stick upon a smoothness in the dust; with words full of the crying of birds and salt in the air and the incessant tumble of it, and now these things came back to me. But I saw that he had been unable to make me, who had always been landlocked, understand the curved spread of the thing, which seemed, at its limit, to pour away into the distance as though endless. I must have lost an hour while I stood and marvelled.

It was an hour I could not afford. Daylight had come and I was exposed by it. The road behind me was now full of vehicles and I knew that inside each vehicle there were eyes. So I crouched low and tried to spy out the land. Along to my right the rocks continued and then, out into the ocean, there was a construction of wood that I saw was a platform for walking upon. There was, I could see, darkness beneath it and I understood that darkness was what I needed.

I stayed under the wharf, which is the name of these platforms, for the rest of the day. It was constructed of great beams of dark wood and I found one which lay just clear of the water and I squatted upon it, and hid.

Beneath my feet the water splashed, making sounds. Sometimes they were the sounds of a mouth. Sometimes it slapped. On occasion the water would jump out from its heaving, green body to splash my feet and I let it. My feet were sore from the trackside gravel and the water soothed them. But it wasn't that. I was full of thoughts. No, not thoughts. I was full of feelings. I was hungry and tired but in truth these feelings were small. The ocean was like a new world that had been given to me and, as though a second moon had appeared in the night, the wonder of it made something in

20

me rise. Against that was the squeeze of knowing that I was gone from the mountain which had always been my home and which had provided for me. What would provide for me now? But these all were small feelings, nothings beside the swelling, pulsing knowledge of the fact that my Daddy lay beneath the ground and would never be there for me to stand beside; would never when I was tired lift me to my horse; would never speak and say, 'Chester, come here,' with a pleasurable lift in his voice as though he was speaking of something that was dear to him.

In the hour before darkness I left the wharf and travelled further along the edge of the land.

I had seen a boat passing on the water and it had been like a miracle. How it moved, swaying gracefully, to this side and that, how it stood upon the water. Inside it there were men and I crouched when I saw them but they didn't see me. Later there were other boats and each one had been utterly pleasurable to gaze upon. The line each boat left in the water, marked in white, became a miracle of healing, like the way the skin repairs itself after a small injury, so that in time there is no trace. The water seemed to be an astonishment, especially when I was so thirsty. Then when I tasted it it was like betrayal—I spat and spat, having nothing to wash the taste away. But this didn't diminish my sense of wonder. The colours. The smell. The birds which played above the waves that broke open upon the strong, broad back of the sand. Of course we had birds upon the mountain—what is a seagull beside an eagle with a twelve-foot span? But seagulls are the air's thoughts made visible.

These were the things which filled my eyes on that first day. As the light began to fade entirely I came upon a wooden boat pulled up upon a beach of golden sand (ah, these words for the first time put to a thing—beach, wave, horizon—such a satisfying feeling). It was tied to a ring set in the rock and I saw that it would not be going anywhere tonight, and had not gone for some time. I got into the boat, which was covered by a stretched blue canvas, and curled myself to the shape of its ribs. And that was the end of my first day in the city called Auckland.

The days which followed were full of rain and I was cold inside my shirt, and always hungry. I ate things that I found on the ground, contested for by wasps and ants, beneath the overflowing rubbish tins which stood on the tufty grass back from the beach. Once a group of men found me and tried to make me go with them. They saw that I was weakened and this enraged them. They pulled my hair and dragged at my arm. But I wriggled free, and ran. My feet were cut and swollen but I forgot that pain in my desire not to be taken. Their black dog chased me and held the tail of my shirt in its teeth, so that it ripped. When I ran the dog came behind, running easily, yipping, circling me. But then I saw it pause and look rearward and realise that its masters were out of sight.

Later I looped back and, following the line of the beach, found my way again to the wooden boat, and climbed into it. What mean things can be made to serve as home.

And yet I knew it would not be my fate to stay there. Now my shirt was ripped, and my feet were causing me to step as though the ground was painful to the touch. Wounded creatures are carried, I knew, by the currents of the world, and so I waited to see where I would be taken.

It was perhaps the fourth day when, late in the morning,

I answered a call of nature by stepping into the ocean. I had waited and waited for a break in the rain, so that my clothes might stay more or less dry, and now I hurried. The air, fresh washed, was golden and my eyes squinted about. Nothing moved and so I went and stood ankle-deep and poured forth my own gold. Then, as I turned away, there came a shout.

'Come here, boy.'

It was a man's voice, deep and strong, and pleasing to obey. Anyone with a brain inside them will know that I heard my father in it. He had always called me to his side in this way and now I went along the beach as though I had no option.

But that is not true. I could have run. I chose to answer that call.

The call had come from the dark rocks which were heaped at one end of the beach and as I went I saw that the man was sitting so still amongst them that a casual glance might not pick him out. He was dark of skin, and his shoulders curved in, as though all his force was being fed into the long line of green which ran away from his index finger. He didn't look up as I approached, but merely spoke. 'Sit down,' he said.

So I sat beside him, and waited.

'If you mimi in the water,' he said, 'all the fishes turn yellow and go off their chop.' While I was considering this he reached down into a bag that was between his feet. He tossed a paper sack to me. I understood I was being given something and I looked inside. Again, sandwiches wrapped in paper. Is this a universal sign, an accessory of the blessed? After I had eaten one, I passed the bag back to him. Seeing this, he turned at last to look at me.

He had a heavy head, marked with lumps, irregular bulges which swelled at his temples. Black hairs twisted forth in patches upon his scalp and also in a ragged moon about his

23

chin. His eyebrows were immense, black, heavy like the bars of a gate. He frowned—they drew up, and I was afraid. But then, as though controlled by his will, the brows settled and into his blue eyes came a mildness that gave the impression that a great being had just sighed away its cares. He grinned down at me, returned the sack with the single remaining sandwich, then found himself an apple in his bag, into which he crunched noisily. When he had finished he drank from a bottle, which we passed back and forth until it was gone. I tried to drink only my share but my thirst was terrible and I am afraid that I failed. This failure was noted by the head, the heavy brows.

Now the line jumped upon the hook of his finger and a ripple went back along it to the water.

The fish was drawn, hand over hand, towards us and then arched upon the sand, flopping in desperation. Tenderly, he beat its brains upon a rock. A pale ribbon of guts was drawn from within it and returned to the waves; scales flew. Then he gathered the line, the bag, his apple core, and, muttering 'Come on, boy,' set off across the grass.

In this manner I was gathered up by his great hand.

He was, I learned, an expert recruiter of boys and dogs, which were equal in his mind: good for fetching newspapers and responding to a whistle; not more. Not things to be spoken to. In truth, only my Daddy ever spoke to me. Even my woman talks in the main with her eyes. But you could sing to dogs; cupping them under the jowls and preventing them from looking away. You could toss dogs a bone and then pretend to take it from them, just to hear the growling. Dogs could warm your feet when your thinking head was in a book; or boys.

His vehicle was an old, hump-backed thing, bottle-green, dust-coated and oily—a Citroën. He opened the passenger's side and, holding the door, flicked with a finger to say I should get in. His head was turned away and his manner impatient but I knew he was noting me carefully and I felt as though I was being drawn into a spiderweb. But I chose to go with him. We drove slowly through the knotted streets and then up the rising curves of roadways that went into the air. There were vehicles everywhere about us, I had never seen so many, but he drove us among them as though he was bored and so I looked out the window without fear. Inside every car there were eyes but I was safe from them now. No horses. No longhorns, no mountain.

No tumbleweed, no cactus, no eagles riding so high you thought that if you kept watching them you would fall over. No dust to work your boots into, no lariat rope inside your hand. The smell of rope and the smell of the dogie as you lay with your weight on top of him and waited for Daddy to come with the hot iron. The ripping smell of the burned hide and the dogie's yelp. No Daddy's voice. No mountain.

We went back among the smaller streets again, then down between two buildings and came to a halt alongside two other vehicles, equally old and saggy, in a little courtyard of gravel surrounded by a high wire fence, topped with barb. He came round, opened the door for me. I had been happy inside the little house of the car and stirred myself with some reluctance. Now that I was at least in some comfort and had eaten and drunk I was able to allow my thoughts to dwell on my bodily state and instantly I was aware of sharp pains in my swollen feet and a great weight which made my bones hard to lift. But he was having none of it. He held the door and regarded the sky as though important things might be seen there while I shifted myself. So I climbed down.

Locking the courtyard with a heavy padlock, he then led me to the back door of a small white building. Inside, a narrow room was provisioned for comfort, with an old couch and a low lamp and music which came from a glowing wooden thing in the corner which I learned to call a radio. Magazines, books. I liked this place at once but was never to enjoy its comfort. Through an open doorway he led me and now I saw we were in some kind of kitchen. There were pots hanging and also baskets of wire. He turned some dials. In two square pools, a dark, heavy liquid waited. A smell of old cooking began to unfold.

He flicked lights on. Down in the corner now a cockroach ran and he said, 'Get him!' I made no move and after a moment he looked thoughtfully down at my feet, too swollen to stamp. 'Use this,' he said, passing me a roll of newspaper. I saw that it had been used for the purpose before; there was a dark stain. 'Those guys are your department.' And he fixed one blue eye on me and secured an answering nod.

Now the square pools were bubbling and his glance warned me away from them. I could feel their heat. Alongside was a flat, black square of metal and from it fumes were rising. He took a small tool and scraped it, all the while that blue eye holding me so that I paid attention. Then he passed the tool and said, 'Like that.' So I began to scrape. There was a thin crust which came away and this was shunted into a gutter. When the gutter was full you cleaned it. You scraped at this square at every moment you weren't doing anything else.

Now he floured the fish he had caught, took a pan and heated it on the black square. He ate from the pan, standing there, slowly, as though he wanted to know each forkful. Now the eye avoided mine. I stood, waiting. I was weary to my bones.

But also excited. This new place was, I could tell from his manner, somewhere where I was going to stay. I heard music coming, sweet and low, from the room through the door; I saw he was listening to it and so I listened too. My Daddy had played me music on an old Victrola with a handle for winding. I didn't know then that I would never be in that comfortable room with the warm light and I was carried away. But the real excitement was from being near him.

Once the fish was done with he again took me up with his eye. Held, I saw how he cleaned the pan, then hung it on a rail where it swung amongst others of its kind. Now he opened a tall white cupboard—of course in time I learned the names of all these things and so I will use them—called a fridge, which breathed out a cloud of frosty air. A patty was laid on the cooking square. Bun halves, cheese. From the fridge he collected a plastic bowl filled with salad. Then, with his holding eye on me, he assembled this into a cheeseburger, bagged it, and passed it to me. It was my first ever and it was entirely delicious.

Now, using a pole, he reached and caught a chain and made it rattle. A metal wall ascended and the front of the kitchen was opened to the early evening air. He placed a wooden box against the side wall and motioned with his finger that I should stand on it. With tender feet, I obeyed. He noted the tenderness. From the box I could see over the front wall of the kitchen: in the street outside, cars were passing. Then I saw a man pass, and another, and I realised that we were open to the world, that breezes were coming in, and that the men could step off their path and come into our place. This was alarming.

He had gone into the back room and now produced a wooden chair which, when placed upon the box and then lifted by books inserted under each leg, made a high seat. He motioned me. 'Okay, Mr Dog,' he said, 'that's where you sit. When someone comes you shout out loud, "Burger time, Mr Stroud!"—got it?'

'Burger time, Mr Stroud.'

'No. Shout it out loud.'

'Burger! Time! Mr! Stroud!'

There followed a period of instruction on the correct way to shout. My Daddy always instructed me—but I think I have said enough about my Daddy. But I was used to being instructed, I liked learning new things, and so when he said, 'You sit there—you don't move—you shout out loud—and you watch everything,' I was happy. I knew what I had to do and that I could do it. He cooked me another cheeseburger, which I ate on my high seat. Men went back and forth across the opening and some of them looked in. Occasionally a man hesitated and I knew it would not be long before one of them stepped off the path and came into our place. Mr Stroud—it was a thing of value, to know his name—went into the back room. I heard him moving there. He turned the radio up and I understood I was also to enjoy the music. My legs were swinging and the music was in my head, and the sound of the radio man talking, and the cars going past, which made a shushing sound, and a kind of humming that was coming from the cooking machines, and my tiredness, and two burgers inside me, and the clean, white light which was falling from the tubes above—all of this was like the components of a happiness I had thought I would never feel again.

And then a creature went past the opening.

I had been listening to the music and perhaps I had drifted off to a distant place where the eagles go when they circle so high. And so I was not really watching. But there had been a creature—inside my head I tried to bring back what had passed before my eyes. A different walk. A different shape. I sat with my head in my hands, trying to remember. Then, sharply, I looked up again. A sound alerted me, a sound from the ground. A clicking. It was going to happen again. And then I saw.

High on my stool, there was no doubt in me. I had seen everything now. It was true. I had seen a woman.

Chapter Three

I wanted to call out to Mr Stroud and discuss this with him. But I knew better. His learn-this eye had told me that my only words were to be the ones he had given me and that transgressions would lead to a more forceful kind of instruction. I had seen how he moved, as though the world had best behave, and I knew this quality and what could flow from it. In horses and in men I had seen this and I kept my boy's mouth shut.

Now a man stepped from the path and came into our light. 'Burger time, Mr Stroud!' I shouted. This caused the man to turn and go back to his path.

When Mr Stroud appeared he took in the situation with a swift, gathering glance. His heavy brows rumpled, and again I was afraid. But again he drew them under his control and when he spoke it was with gentleness. 'It's like fishing,' he said. He was looking out into the evening and he spoke low, so that I had to strain. This was, I knew, a trick to get me to listen good—and also to quieten those forces in him which wanted to beat the world into shape. My Daddy did that. 'You sit and you don't eyeball them,' said Mr Stroud. 'They know you're there. They have to step into the light and it makes them jumpy. But they settle. You watch and you'll see them be ready. That's when you shout—okay, Mr Dog?'

And he shook his fingers in my hair.

The shock that he had touched me was so great that I almost forgot what I had seen. Almost. It was a rare day when my Daddy's hand was on me. Sometimes he would bump me as he passed in the close of the sleepout, though this was uncommon; Daddy had control. Afterwards I would study the glow which came from the place. If he was content, say after a successful day in the saddle, we would squat side by side and look out over the sunset lands—then his hand might come up and rest on my shoulder. He might say, 'Hey, Chester.' If there was dirt in my eye he apologised before he took hold of my head. It was the same with the horses or his favourite dog. His hands were what he made the world with and they should be saved for that, for making, and so when they were at rest they held each other, keeping their power holstered. Sometimes a horse would lean on him and he would allow this. Horses feel what's inside you and sometimes they want what you have. He would pat the horses, if they had done good.

But his fingers had never been in my hair and as Mr Stroud went back to his comfortable room my eyes followed him. And I was thinking.

It had been such a time for me, since I left the mountain. I had rode on a train, I had seen the ocean. I had tasted cheeseburger. And now. Sitting on my high chair, under the electricity of the light tube, in the buzzing of the machines, with the music playing, inside my tiredness—sitting high up there I saw that I had no reason to hold my head in my hands. And so I sat and tried to see what might be seen.

Two men crossed the threshold and stood in our light. They were wearing peaked caps with writing and their eyes were back in shadow. I waited, just looking off to the side as when you first spy a dogie in the brush, and this was successful. They looked about freely and then one made a passing glance at me. So I spoke up: 'Burger time, Mr Stroud,' and this was rightly judged. From his room he appeared and said, 'Hi.'

I saw how, even now, he gave them time. His hands rested on his belly, which was large and shaped for that, and his gaze moved over the surface of his countertop as though he was musing on what had been placed there. And so they released their orders from where they had been building up inside and he took these and began to cook.

I tried to follow his hands but it was like trying to keep your eye on a bird when there is a flock in flight, they moved here and there, placing, taking, and everything they touched was obedient. Mr Stroud never hurried but the food was shortly assembled, each piece given a bag, and passed over in exchange for coins and notes. My Daddy had showed me about money. Mr Stroud had a drawer which came out like a tongue without his hands touching—I didn't see how this was done. But I knew that he had thought about this and made this piece of the world as he needed it. He had done the same with the men. They had been made by the way he spoke only a few words to them, and with the language of his bent back, the inclination of his head. He made it so they did what he wanted; he had made them like him.

A man crossed our threshold on his own, and then two more; then two together, then one, then three. One of the three was a boy and I leaned forward in my chair so that I might see him over the countertop—at once Mr Stroud stilled his hands and his eye came speedily to me, so that I settled back.

Then two women. It was really true; there were women here.

They were young, though older than me, and they laughed at everything that they saw, mouths open. One was dark-skinned like Mr Stroud, but it was skin like I had never seen and I could not take my eyes off its loveliness. But it wasn't just her skin. The woman-ness of her was just there about her for anyone to see and I was utterly filled by a desire to speak to her. But she spoke first, she said to Mr Stroud, who too late I realised had been eyeing me, and she said, 'Your boy's got binoculars up his bum.'

Again Mr Stroud was gentle. He smiled carefully at me and said, low, 'Mr Dog.' And I withdrew my eyes to myself.

Where should I look? I tried to look at the floor. A cockroach ran and my hand moved towards the newspaper but Mr Stroud's head inclined slightly in my direction and my hand went back to my lap. So I found that space in the air that Mr Stroud himself gazed into, which was an invisible hole where distant voices could be heard. When the young women were gone he turned to me and gave me a strange little smile. 'Good boy, Mr Dog,' he said, and went back to his room and his music.

And so the evening passed and my eyes were filled with things that might be clearly seen only when I was looking into the hole which stood in the air before me. Looking there I saw now the second woman who had accompanied the one who spoke about me. This woman had skin with a pale golden cast to it, and dark hair, and her eyes went sideways. I have heard these eyes called slits but these were no slits. In that hole I heard my Daddy talking and finally now his words made sense to me. 'Women make the head of a man so filled with stars that he don't know which one to follow,' he would say. And I, who had seen stars but never a woman, would gaze up into the black of night and see something that shined harder after you looked away.

After some hours set high up there upon the chair my legs began to ache and so I stepped down and began to pace. Mr Stroud was in his comfortable room and I remembered how nice it was there and so I went in to join him. 'Back!' he called from his chair, 'Back! Back!' I retreated until my toes were beyond the join where the floor-covering changed colour. There was a thin strip of shining metal and my toes were not to touch it.

There I stood, shifting quietly from foot to foot, feeling the blood tingling and also the cuts which stung like lashes from a little whip. The music played. There were colours in its sounds, deep blues and pale pinks, and then a voice or voices which swam about my head. They sang of faraway places, of shrimp boats acomin' and an island of dreams—words which made pictures that tilted slightly before my eyes, back and forth like the ocean which had tossed beneath my feet when I was under the wharf and hiding. I did not mind that I could not enter Mr Stroud's comfortable room, I was sure I would go there some day, and so I shifted from foot to foot and let those singing voices make tilting pictures in my head. And thus I fell to the floor.

Mr Stroud carried me outside. I looked up and saw his face against the night lights, studying me as I was in his arms and through my faint I felt a smile come to my lips. He placed me in the vehicle, along the length of the rear seat, and drew a blanket over me. From inside the kitchen I heard a cry of 'Shop!' but he tended to me without pause. Once I was comfortably laid out he went to the front of the vehicle, where he opened a small cupboard, the glovebox, and found some smooth cream, which he applied to my feet. It stung, but I knew he was being kind and I made no murmur. Before he closed the vehicle's door he opened its window and so I was able, faintly, to still hear that music which came from his small room with its low light and waiting chair. It sang of blue moons and summer places and ghost riders in the sky. Yippie-i-oh, yippie-i-ay. And so I went under.

Later I heard the engine start and through the night we travelled. Out the window now I could see stars tumbling and wheeling and I felt my life go tumbling too. Inside me there was a long hollow shape that was where my Daddy had been, and it seemed as though it had been a thousand days since I had held in my arms his body broken open to the blood inside. But it had not been a thousand; only five, perhaps.

But I was only a boy of twelve years and my head was loaded with so many new things, signs and wonders, and if it is not true to say that the hollow was filled by these things—the women; the cheeseburgers—then I can only say that further room was made inside me, to accommodate. And so I travelled, and understood that we had stopped. Mr Stroud silenced the engine, then stepped around to adjust the windows of the car. 'You sleep now, Mr Dog,' he said. 'If you have to mimi, get out and go on the ground. Don't go wandering.' After which he was gone.

I heard a door shut, then silence. And so I slept.

When I awoke the sun was high in the sky and air in the vehicle was hot. Sitting up, I looked around and saw an enclosed yard, with browned grass that was ready for grazing, and a high fence. Across the yard was a wire on which a figure was pegging out bedclothes. Mr Stroud. I watched him and understood from the shape of his back that I should not call out to him. I remembered how sometimes my Daddy was like this, turned away, and I sat in the vehicle and waited. When he completed his work he came towards me, and saw me, I felt his eyes catch me, but he made no sign. There was a large white dwelling and he opened its door and went inside it.

I did as he had told me and got out to answer my call of nature. My feet were still tender, but they did not sting so sharply. The air was warm, close, and loaded with those tiny particles which made my eyes strain, as though I was trying to see between them. My business was soon completed but then I stood in the air, taking a small liberty. There was noise all around, voices in the distance, and the sound of vehicles, but nothing close. Beyond the fence I saw roofs in every direction and realised that there were many dwellings here and that this was the part of the city where all the people lived—that there were lives in profusion here. But they could not be seen. Nothing could be seen, because of the fence, which was high and made of old iron, faded red in colour and peeling, with waves in it which stood upright, held by nails. Within this, the yard was a little world and I saw that Mr Stroud liked these little worlds where none could enter. I studied his dwelling, which was constructed in an ingenious fashion—boards had been laid lengthwise along its side, each board above overlapping the one below it. Each board was painted white. There was pipe work and, around the roof, a metal rim; everything in white. My eye followed this and saw how, if it rained, the water would be channelled and this was the same, I understood, as the wooden channels which had carried the water away from the roof of the sleepout on the mountain.

Busy with mapping the system of water management, I did not hear any sounds that might have occurred. I had stepped away from the vehicle and was halfway along one side of Mr Stroud's building when I realised that a terrible low growling had for some moments been coming from behind me. At one time I was closed upon in this way by a lynx and then jumped when Daddy shot it dead right at my heel. Now I turned slowly. An immense dog had its mouth held

36

half open, so that its fangs could be glimpsed—the growling came from deep in its throat. Just as it was about to spring at me, a window of the house opened and Mr Stroud shouted down, 'Blackie!' so that the dog cowered, and slunk away. I saw now that it was not so large as I had imagined.

Mr Stroud glared down, at the dog and also at me. But I had done no wrong that I could think of and so I stood in my ragged clothing and waited. He saw this and one dark eyebrow lifted. We gazed at each other and it passed between us that it was he who had brought me here, that I had no clue as to where I might be and that all the running was with him. In my mind I was shaping words which might politely express this—as soon as he saw that I was about to speak he hurried to say, 'Okay, come round to the door.'

When the door opened I moved forward but he held me with an upraised hand. He passed a plastic bottle of water—I had never seen plastic before—and a bag which proved to have two sandwiches inside. Then the door was closed on my face.

As I sat eating upon the step, the dog Blackie came up, wagging his tail, and I gave him a portion of the sandwich I was eating. Thus that dog and I became friends and whenever I was in the yard belonging to Mr Stroud I talked to him as though he was a boy my own age.

Looking up, I saw that Mr Stroud had the window open and had observed my gift.

Soon the door opened again and he passed out to me a bundle, which proved to be clothes. They were worn and faded as though many summers and winters had passed through them. But they were more or less my size. And there were underdrawers and socks, which were garments I had often done without. The shoes were of the kind I discovered were called tennis shoes, in white, and, dressed in these items,

I felt I had now become part of the city and should soon feel at home here. I wandered about Mr Stroud's yard, with the dog Blackie at my heel, and stared. The grass was patchy and, looking down, my eyes found a cloudscape with my white tennis shoes in it. There were cloudscapes to be found also in the peeling paint of the fence metal. This world was so close to you, I seemed to be seeing through it to a horizon. But the city was a flat place with no mountain.

The vehicle standing on its square of grey concrete, dripping oil; the line made by the top of the fence as it ran away towards the road; the lines in the air made by birds as they flew low across that walled-in space of Mr Stroud's: I stood in the middle of that oblong yard, with the sound made by the flapping bedclothes, with the dog Blackie standing just where my fingers might feel among the stiff hairs at its collar, and tears flowed down my cheeks. Looking up, I saw Mr Stroud on the other side of a panel of window glass. He was watching me steadily.

At dusk we again drove through the city to the burger bar and once again I took my place on the chair held high by the quartet of books.

And so began the first of many nights at the burger bar which, in time, I came to know as I Fry, and which, for a while, was all the home I had in the world. I was permitted that night, or perhaps it was the next, to cook my own burger, with Mr Stroud grunting behind me, and smoke rising from the grill-plate and the dreamy music coming just faintly from the comfortable room which was just through the wall. In time I learned to hold a paper bag open at the right angle so that Mr Stroud could slip a fresh-cooked burger inside. I learned to cut salad and to peel cheese slices. I kept the salt shaker topped up and also made sure its holes were unclogged. It was always nice to pour salt.

I learned not to stare at the customers, even if they were women, but to know from the small movements of their heads and shoulders what their desires might be. I learned that, no matter how hungry you were, you could never eat while the front of the bar was open.

I learned to shout 'Burger time, Mr Stroud' in a manner that I now understand was a little theatrical.

I learned to move in the narrow space behind the counter at the same time that Mr Stroud was moving in it so that we never touched one another and so that the boiling oil never splashed and so that my hands never became entangled with his hands as they assembled the food. It was possible, I discovered, to say nothing during the assembly of one hundred burgers. To never so much as catch an eye. The floor was spread with springy rubber and the light back in the kitchen area so soft, I now saw, that the eyes were always rested and easy there. The radio sang its song. But, as the burger count rose, a tension would slowly form in me. At first I would notice it in my stomach and in the early days I thought it was hunger, though I always started each evening with at least one burger with everything. Then I thought that I was worried: that the radio would fail. But why would it fail? But I realised that I was listening. In time I managed to control this tension, to keep it from going into my hands, which had to be close to his but to never touch. I would rest on my high chair and listen to my breath, which seemed to come loudly into me. Then—usually after a late crowd had been dispatched into the warm night, their voices fading, and the radio again could be heard—then, as I climbed back to my chair, he would say, as he passed on his way back to his room, 'Good boy, Mr Dog,' and I would let out the long breath I had been holding in and go back to my study of that hole in the air which held in it everything in the world that mattered.

Sometimes his fingers would stir my hair, and once, when I burned myself with a splash of oil, he took hold of my hand and soothed it with a white cream that took all the pain away. His careful, strong fingers, circling on the back of my hand, which he was holding. If they could sell his fingers with every tube of that cream there would be a line waiting for it that went all the way to the horizon.

Chapter Four

It was at the end of that night, or perhaps the next, that I saw he was making it his business to keep his eyes from me, as though I had made a terrible mistake that could not be mentioned. Did he always clean up like this, with his head down? Everywhere I looked I saw his back.

Finally he did look at me. We were out in the night now, standing in the wire cage where his vehicle was parked; he turned and said, 'Okay, Mr Dog—see you tomorrow.'

Then he turned away.

The engine of his vehicle came to life and he drove forward a little, then, while I watched, hefted the steering wheel so that the black tyres worked harshly against the gravel below. It was a sound that was terrible to me. When he drove backwards, the tyres passed within an inch of my toes— jumping clear, I saw him eyeing me through the windscreen from beneath the dark of his brows and I thought he would run me down. It was night and where should I go, in that wire cage? I knew that to depart he would have to unlock it. Should I allow myself to be locked in? Or, while the big gate was open, should I run? I could, I thought, climb the fence. But the barb at the top would tear my new clothes.

And in a trice I was torn from the small comfort I had gathered in the night or two with him and carried back to that moment on the mountainside when the bullet came from the gun of the coward Stronson, who had concealed himself behind a cactus. There he stood in the open—should I take my father's guns and return his fire? Or tend to my father, whose chest now had a violent opening in it? Or run? I hated Mr Stroud for making me know that moment again, though it is true that I will never unknow it.

My Daddy was falling and what should I do?

As his will abandoned him he made a last effort and turned on his heel. Or was this the force of that tiny flying length of lead? A twist of pain? Whatever it was, as he fell it seemed that he threw himself round so as to face the coward; but fell back. And I could do nothing but catch him. The weight was so great that I staggered and together we went down. Blood ran from his mouth and then his eyes went away.

Like a dark bird speeding low over the lands towards the sun, his eyes went away from me.

With footsteps that crunched slowly in the gravel of the mountainside the coward Stronson now came. His shadow fell across me, and across the body of my Daddy; standing over us, he spoke down. But I was following that dark bird and could not hear. My arms held my Daddy and I knew that if I once laid him down I would never have him again. And so I held his heavy body there on the mountainside, knowing that the bird of him was gone, and sounds came out of me that I had no power over. Whose body I had never held. Whose dark blood I had never seen. Those terrible sounds are all that I or anyone who goes to that place will ever hear.

The vehicle was correctly positioned now before the gate, which was open, and its engine was running. Mr Stroud weighed the padlock in his hand and then he turned to me. I was standing in the night as though I no longer knew how to move. He said, 'Where you gonna go, Mr Dog?'

42

He spoke roughly and once the words were out I saw that he was controlling himself. I saw how he directed the great force of himself so that nothing would come to harm. I said, 'I'll go to my boat.' And I held his eye and made him responsible. 'Please point me to the way.'

'I'll take you down there,' he said.

Which ended his responsibility to me and so I nodded. Though I was full of despair.

He saw all of this. His hand continued to weigh the padlock as though it was something he wanted to fling from him. His head came up and then his eyes travelled slowly towards the night above us; my own eyes followed, as he intended they would. I saw the stars, which give comfort only if you have no need of it. His feet made a sound, they crunched in the gravel as he came towards me. That terrible crunching—I made myself stand steady. But he wasn't coming to me. To the side of the white-painted burger bar—all of his buildings were white—he went and placed one hand on something that was there. Into something. In the wall, I saw this now, was a vertical line of indentations, also painted white and thus all but invisible. He glanced round, checking that we were not observed. 'Up you go,' he said.

As soon as I began climbing he went to his vehicle. He drove it through the gates. If I was quick I might have descended and run free. But I saw that he wasn't trying to race me.

When the vehicle was out he came back for the padlock. 'Hurry up,' he said, gesturing me forward with a hand. Then he was gone.

The rooftop of the I Fry burger bar was where I spent that night and, for some time, all of the nights that followed. In a heap there I found a waterproof canvas covering and, beneath the canvas, a folded length of foam and a bedroll.

What did it mean that he had admitted me to this part of his world? But I had discovered that what Mr Stroud meant by anything was not easy to guess. As I bundled the bedroll about me I went inside the smell of his body, which had been here. Other bodies too, and dogs. Above, the stars now looked close.

I had often slept out under the stars with my Daddy and was familiar with the way they pressed down upon you. Not at first. But when in the night you wake their bright spots are burned on the inside of your head and blinking them away does no good. The sensation that an immense universe had entered you and was swirling there was so overwhelming that at times my stomach felt twisted by it. And thus I felt now; as though my eyes had seen things that my body struggled to contain.

But yet it was warm inside that bedroll.

Sleeping out on the mountainside you heard the occasional moan of a cattlebeast, or coyotes. But these were single events which broke the spread of the silence; which hung in the night, and then faded. In the city, now, there was no silence. The rushing sound of vehicles was always there, that grinding they make which rose and fell but never died away. As I lay I began to think of the men inside the vehicles, which journeyed through the night. Did they never lie down? Where at this hour were they going?

And footsteps, and voices. Men talking, though what they said could never be discerned. The words sank into the low growl of the city sound and that was true of everything here, the way that one piece of the world ran into another and there were no boundaries. Shouting, which died down. And, from time to time, the voices of women.

Lying out with my Daddy I would listen to him explain what women would one day mean to me and all the wonder of the stars seemed a small thing beside. 'The day will come,' he would say, 'when you look at the mountain and think of her. You will see her in the way your horse walks, and you will smell her in the smell of your lariat, and you will look out over the lands and not see anything but her, everywhere you look and nowhere that can be seen. I once rode forty-four mile, Chester, across country so broken and bad that only the gophers cared to plant a stake there, and at the end I got not so much as a look. Every mile I heard her name coming across the lands like the winds was trying to tell me somethin'; and they was. That was the thing, boy: they was.'

I would lie, frowning, with those stars just burning in my face, and try to make a picture of this that made sense. I could see my Daddy on his horse, crouched low and going fast, and I could see the badlands. But the why? I heard him give a great sigh in the dark and tried to think what he might be feeling. 'What was her name?' I would say.

'I used to ask myself that,' he said. 'What was her right name?' And then nothing further, though I would wait and wait. The picture of him riding now had him listening to the wind for a name that he didn't know and I pictured his ear, which I knew to be sharp, listening out over the sound of the horse's hooves, the horse's breathing, and hearing nothing, only the wind.

Or we would be squatted under the noonday sun alongside a tether pole for the horses and he would draw in the dust, anatomical pictures that he would make and then scrub away with his boot. 'Those are the facts, boy,' he would say, 'and they tell you precisely nothin'.' But you have to know 'em, just like you have to know that your beasts could do with some salt, if only there was a lick of salt to be found.' And he would stare out over the lands as though trying to catch sight of that one unbranded cow that always managed to hide up when the iron was hot. And I would stare too, trying to see what he could not.

The roof of the I Fry burger bar had a low rim around it and this gave shelter from any wind, and also from the edge of the city sounds. But there was a clicking, and when I lifted my head to look on the front of the building I saw mounted an arrangement of glass tubes with bright colour inside, which clicked on and then off. This, I discovered, was called neon and its colour was like seeing the soft inside of something, the colour of a promise being delivered. It was through this colour, repeatedly offered and then taken back, that I looked down at the walk and saw the heads of those who instead of sleeping were acquainted with the night. The tubes of light cast livid colour on their faces that made them seem like figures from a dream come to inform you of the state of your soul.

If the night was especially still and if he seemed disposed I would summon the courage to say, 'Daddy, tell me again 'bout my Mama.' But not too often, as this always occasioned a great sigh. His voice would come rising from within his chest and hang in the night. Even the stars listened. On the mountainside at night there are only a few sounds, a little run in the red gravel, the footfall of a mouse, and every living thing there stills its breathing to lean in and catch the meaning. On the down slope, the faint rustle of owl feathers; and my Daddy's rumble as he gets the words out. 'Her eyes was so green that when finally you tore yourself 'way from 'em the whole world looked as though it was painted in cactus. Those damn eyes, Chester, I jest always was wanting in be in 'em.' Ah, I would think, her eyes were *green*. And I would adjust the picture I had of her, which was no picture at all but something you knew must be there, from feeling it, like the skin of your back. She was on my skin, she was in me, but I had no idea of her and, with the death of my Daddy, never would now have an idea.

Or so I thought.

But I knew she was purty—so wondrously purty. I knew she had dark curls that twisted like a riverside trail. I knew she smelled like the freshest summer day there ever was, like just a field of rippling wheat, like the warmest wind that ever blew out of the west and ruffled your hair and told you 'bout wonderful things that were blowin' your way. All of this my Daddy gave to me and every word of it I squirrelled away good. But my Mama herself, she was hidden from me.

These were among the things passing through my mind as I lay within the low wooden rim of the roof and listened to the night city.

And then slept.

Thus my first days in the city unfolded. I slept under the canvas if it rained and woke with a thick head. But it was late summer and mostly the air was hot and I slept out in it. I would watch the light come and only when the sun was shining full down on me would I rise. I had never stayed in my bedding so late. But there was nothing to rise for.

Some slow wisdom was guiding me, then. I seemed to know that this was a healing time—that I was being fed and sheltered, that my feet were healing, that I should rest while I could as the days ahead might be broken lands that I had to cross. I lay low within the wooden rim and looked at what could be seen. But I was cautious. Mr Stroud had given me the understanding that the roof was a secret place that none should know of.

Great airplanes flew over me, wing tips flashing.

In the evenings Mr Stroud's vehicle would come growling to the wire gate and my day would change. Quickly I would descend, carrying the plastic holder into which I made my water, and would be gestured on into the building's interior, and fed. Sometimes Mr Stroud brought the dog Blackie to sit beside my high chair, but low, out of sight. Mr Stroud would allow me to have the company of the dog for an hour or two and then he would call, from his comfortable room, and the dog would pad away, leaving me with just the radio for company, and my heart would follow the dog and wish I might have him back, or go with him, or be him, lying with Mr Stroud's feet on my belly and the soft light from the low lamps falling. But the radio was always there.

In time I heard songs from the radio that I had heard before and my hands would grip the base of the chair and I would rock while tears came streaming down my face. To be known by a song, to have in your body the path that it will follow; to travel with it as it takes the path, every word falling reliably into the place that it fell before—ah, this is the greatest comfort. Sometimes Mr Stroud would call out, 'You're killing the chickens, Mr Dog!' and I would realise that I had been singing—moaning!—along with the words. Sometimes the dog Blackie would strike up, yowling in accompaniment from his place by my feet and be scolded by Mr Stroud, and everyone would quieten down. But the radio went on, always there, always singing. Even today I can hear those songs that it sang, I know every word and as I ride the cactus-thick slopes I sing to the horse and we clip-clop along in a dream.

This was among my favourites.

I gotta go down, go diving in the bay
Gotta get a lot of oysters, find some pearls today
To make a pretty necklace for Leah
Lee-ee-ah.

I saw myself diving deep into the blue waters of the ocean, amid the miles of gorgeous colour stretched everywhere around, and looking among the giant clams for the pearl to bring to the woman Leah. Of course I could not swim, and cannot even today, but these are facts which do not count when you are inside the world of the radio—miles of gorgeous colour.

But something's wrong, I cannot move around
My leg is caught, it's pulling me down
But I'll keep my hands shut tight for if they find me
They'll find the pearl for Leah.

These words I would whisper to myself and with each word that fell my feelings would rise. Rocking on my high chair, I felt that every moment of my past was being spoken of, was known; that I myself was known, that somewhere my future was known, and that there was no reason to despair. Thus I never wanted any song to end. And yet after each song there was another and once I realised this and knew that for the rest of my life it would be true I felt my burdens lift and a strange gladness entered me that has never faded.

The evening came when Mr Stroud padded to the door on silent feet and I opened my eyes to find him studying me. My cheeks were wet and I was ashamed. 'The music is talking to you, Mr Dog,' he observed. He crossed the metal line in the floor to stand beside my high chair and put an arm around me; this made the tears flow more thickly. His fingers went into my hair and stirred my head about. He held me tightly. From his comfortable room the radio played a song that I knew and the words were filled with him standing there beside my chair and holding me and now as I sing them I can feel his great arm across my back.

> *We traded my last cigarette*
> *Blew hearts into the night*
> *Yours drifted into nothingness*
> *Mine wouldn't come out right*
> *Beyond the curtained window*
> *The city couldn't sleep*
> *It was the season of the restless*
> *When promises are cheap.*

> *Yeah, the season of the faithless*
> *Of orange traffic lights*
> *Of cars with motors running*
> *Of strings that broke on kites*
> *That's when I knew I loved you*
> *In the season of the fool*
> *You were always leaving*
> *In the season of the fool.*

> *Yeah, you were always leaving*
> *Me to walk the night alone*
> *In the city of the sleepless*
> *Of the ever-ringing phone*
> *I walk down by the river*
> *Where all the lovers go*
> *I see their traded hearts*
> *And wonder, do they know?*

That in the season of the faithless
Which soon must come around
All the midnight trains are leaving
And broken hearts abound
In the city of the sleepless
In the suburbs of the heart
The seasons turn to winter
When everyone must part.

Yeah, the season of the faithless
In the hardest of all schools
Where all the streets are lonely
And the lovers all are fools.

That night he took me home with him and gave me a small room inside his house to sleep in, with fresh bedding and a soft pillow for my head.

In the morning he sent me out to give Blackie his bone. As I went back inside Blackie followed, but only to the threshold, which he knew his feet must not cross. We ate breakfast with the door open, Mr Stroud cooking, me at the table, Blackie lying in a circle on the mat. Bacon and eggs, just like my Daddy made. Then, on a good day, fishing, from a boat, that stood upon the water with me inside it. I was afraid, and yet filled with wonder. Mr Stroud saw that I was astonished and said, 'You can put your hand in.' So I trailed a hand. But the feeling that some dripping monster would rise and bite was too great. Mr Stroud saw this and I saw him looking at me all over again.

I was used to washing myself at the burger bar but at his home Mr Stroud ran me a bath, which was soapy and smooth and made my skin feel as though it had never had a speck of dust on it. And new clothes—in truth, old clothes, again, but new-washed and new to me. A shirt with palm trees on it, and islands.

That night when the kitchen of the burger bar was cleaned he turned to me and said, 'So, darling Dog.'

He had one hand on his hip, making an elbow; this was a game, I could see that from his face. Trying to play it right, I said, 'So, Mr Stroud.' Which felt good; it was what I would have said to my Daddy.

Mr Stroud grinned. 'I thought so,' he said. And we both laughed, though I didn't know what we were laughing at. I followed him outside, where he paused; looking up, he said, 'It's a great night for it.' Which was true, there was a round moon that filled your head with light. 'I envy you,' he said. And he jumped into his vehicle and drove to the gate.

When he was outside he came back for the padlock. I was standing with my feet in the crunchy gravel, watching. I was hearing that song and again near to tears. He swung the gate into place, locked it, then stood looking at me through the mesh. 'Mr Dog,' he called. My eyes went to him but my feet didn't move. 'Come here, Mr Dog.'

At the gate it was as though the mesh was a mask, all I could see through it were his eyes, which were dark and full of moon. His head was huge, moon-blown. He was laughing at me. All I could hear was that song. I didn't feel like laughing. But Mr Stroud was making me; through the mesh I could feel him making me laugh. So I laughed.

It made me a bit angry, and I turned away. But he called after me. 'What's your name, Mr Dog?'

'Chester,' I said angrily.

'Chester,' he said, sounding the word as though it was strange to him. 'Chester Dog,' he said.

'No, it's Chester Farlowe.'

52

'Chester Farlowe, Mr Dog. Very good. I'm Henry,' he said. 'Pleased to meet you, Mr Dog.' And he wagged his fingers at me through the mesh. So I went back over there, as he wanted me to, and stood looking at his fingers. He was looking at them too. Only one was waggling now and eventually I took it between my finger and thumb and shook it. As he wanted me to. I was still a little bit angry. But balanced against that was that he had given me his name, which was something he could never now take back.

'Listen, Mr Dog,' he said, and he poked a key through the mesh. 'It's the only one I have. So you have to be here at opening time to let me in, okay?'

'Okay, Henry,' I said.

'Mr Stroud to you, boy,' he said. But he was joking and I couldn't resist him; he had made me happy, and I laughed.

Then he jumped into his vehicle and, toot-toot, drove away.

Every time I woke in the night the moon was there, looking down on me as though I was a profound curiosity; and I felt the key inside my fist. Then when I woke it was daylight and I knew it was time for me to go and explore the city.

But I did not.

Instead I sat amongst the bedding and let the sun beat down on me. I listened. In the night I had heard wolves howling and I wasn't in any hurry to find myself where they might be. I had at that time never seen a wolf and when I thought of them I felt the absence of a gun or protection of any kind. And my stomach was empty—how could I walk out into a strange place on an empty stomach? Thoughts of this sort came into my head and I said them over to myself, enjoying their self-evident truth.

I went to the wooden rim of the roof and studied the traffic. Vehicles came and went, of every type of manufacture. My father had told me of the immense factories where such things were forged but I had always found this somehow too much to imagine. He had pointed me to the black highway which crossed the edge of our lands and sometimes we discussed the vehicles that were passing there. 'They travel between the great cities,' he told me, 'they flow like blood all over the land,' and this I had seen with my own eyes. But I had never believed, not really. The black highway had been, like the River of Jordan, something that could be talked about by men of intelligence; but not anything you would ever see, or touch. And now I had travelled upon it, myself. And now I was seeing the vehicles, which came without pause along the flat road—Jervois Road, its name was, in the region called Ponsonby—and as I studied them it occurred to me that everything my Daddy had told me was true. This was a notion so troubling that I held my poor head between my hands and tried to cool the lava that was bubbling within it. This meant that here there would be houses where great stories were told in pictures up upon a coloured wall, and elephants and giraffes, and men with skin so black that it shone, and pygmy men, and giants, and tall narrow buildings that pointed to the sky where room upon room was piled up until you were at the height of the clouds. I had never credited what my Daddy had seen and had been always content with our lives on the mountain, and now, as the vehicles streamed towards me without ever repeating themselves, I saw that it must be true about the immense factories. I fell back in a kind of horror, and lay amongst my bedding. Every time I opened my eyes the sun was directly above me, a burning ball that could not be denied—and then I remembered that this sun was, according to my Daddy, standing still in the sky and that we, on a ball of our own, were travelling around it. All of this was now true to me. And yet it was too much to be true—that there would be great emporiums where everything in the world could be bought. This had been a game we played: 'So could I buy . . .' I would say, 'a python snake as long as four horses?' He would nod and then smile at me, because I was laughing. Now I saw the true nature of his smile, which had borne an indulgence in which I had always bathed.

A great airplane passed low overhead and I saw that this must be real, that there must really be men inside it.

I sat amongst my bedding and held my head, and so the day passed. At the edge of my thoughts I heard a sound and when it was repeated, toot-toot, I scrambled down the side of the building to turn the key in the jigsaw hole of the padlock. As the vehicle passed into the wire compound, I saw him in there and remembered that I knew his name. 'Henry Stroud,' I said, and was pleased with myself.

He stood in the gravel, smiling at me. 'And where have you been, my blue-eyed son?'

His fond attention was something so blissful that I just stood there swaying. But he was in fact interested and so I told him. I said, 'I went down by the ocean,' I said, 'and I studied the creatures. I walked along the oceanside and there was a factory where they make vehicles and buildings that go up to the sky and a wild elephant with swaying tusks and an airplane and every kind of man,' I said. 'And little horses that are too small even to be ponies and red fire engines and women and millions of men all fearsome busy without one of 'em knowing how to so much as milk a cow when they're wantin' for a drink,' I said.

'Is that right, Mr Dog,' he said.

'The name is Chester.' I had heard my Daddy use this formulation, once.

'Okay, Mr Dog,' he said, and went inside to turn on the equipment.

All that evening I saw he was watching me, as he had at the first, which I didn't enjoy, it made it hard to go inside the music, and I heard myself shouting out my words, 'Burger time, Mr Stroud!' instead of just producing them unknowing, and instead of his fond regard I felt the burden of being studied. Then, late, he turned the music off. This was unprecedented. I looked to see if we were closing but, no, here we had an action out of sequence. He appeared at the door of the comfortable room and leaned against its frame, regarding me. I tried to enjoy this. I regarded him back, but that was too hard, he was too much for that, so I looked at the hole in the air which was where I spent most of the burger-bar evenings. But all I could see was the floor splattered with the ancient spillage of cooking. Not that there was much, Mr Stroud was very deft. But I saw the actual substance of that place, which was somewhat grubby.

'So, Mr Dog,' he said. 'What d'you know?'

'Chester,' I said.

'Okay, darling Dog,' he said. He saw me scowl at him, so he said, 'Chester.' But I knew he didn't mean it. His big shoulder was heavy against the door frame and, against his white apron, his brown hands were the size of horses' heads, long and weighty. Yet he could move them so clever. He was bigger than my Daddy, a giant, though sometimes he kept this bigness to himself. But the biggest thing was his head, which was all bumped about and scarred from having too much inside it, the moon and all the songs on the radio and everything he'd ever seen. The dark skin of it was tight, as though it was still growing, with tufty bits of black hair like vegetation clinging to a desperate hillside. His gaze was a swaying ocean.

'You a farm boy, Chester?'

'From the red dirt lands,' I said. 'Around the mountain.'

'Cows?'

'Cattle,' I said, nodding.

'Horses?'

I nodded at this fool question.

'You can ride a horse?'

I didn't know how to answer this; I looked at him, and I guess there must have been some kind of appeal in my eyes, for he put out one of his great hands and messed up my hair. My head tilted so that he could get his fingers in properly and to my amazement he came closer and he stroked my head and my ears and the upper part of my back. 'Eh, Mr Dog,' he said. 'You like that.' I couldn't speak. But I managed to nod. His arm went around me and pressed me to his side and I leaned into him. 'Mr Dog,' he said. 'Somebody hurt you?'

I considered this. Finally I shook my head.

There was a customer came at that moment and so he released me. But before his arm went away it gave me a little squeeze and that squeeze filled me with feeling. Yes, a good feeling. But also in it was that he would return. That he would come back and look at me and ask more questions.

Chapter Five

One morning as I was stretching away the cares of the night I heard a familiar sound: toot-toot. It would be several hours, I knew, before the I Fry might begin the warming of the hotplates, but, with its front that appeared to be frog lips pressed against the mesh of the gate, there was the green Citroën with Henry Stroud at the wheel. He had his head out the window and was looking up at me. On the other side, the dog Blackie too had his head out and was barking excitedly.

We proceeded among the morning traffic—past lights that changed colour, across thick white stripes painted on the road. These were, I knew, signs and were speaking as signs speak. But I did not know their language. There were men everywhere but Henry paid them no mind. He whistled as his hands managed the steering wheel and seemed carefree. But I knew that he was watching me.

On the streets of the city were buildings which faced each other and we passed steadily between. The buildings seemed to be calling out, as though they wanted us; there were openings in their front sides and men were going in. Women also. Yes, there were women everywhere, young women, old ones bent over, girls running freely as though no one was in control of them. Looking at the girls made me so happy.

No horses. But my Daddy had told me that. 'They have girls instead a horses, if you seen a colt runnin' you seen a girl, an' there's one there somewheres for evry boy.' But he always said this with a twinkle in his eye and I had always thought he was teasing me.

And no open spaces. Everywhere my eye went there was something that arose in front of it. Tall poles and wires across the sky. I felt then the way the city presses upon you. What I could see was too much for me to ever know about, but the press was like thumbs upon your temples: the knowledge that behind everything you could see there was more, and more, always going on; the knowledge was that you couldn't see it, would never see it, but would always have to know it was there. Whereas on the mountain I could pronounce the name of each thing my eye rested upon.

I was happy that we were inside the little world of the vehicle.

Henry drove us along a great street and then down a hill so steep that I thought I would fall into it through the front window. He guided the car to the edge of the black roadway and silenced its engine. Now we were in the middle of many sounds. 'Sit, Blackie,' he said, and the dog, who had been between my knees, settled upon the floor. Henry came round, holding my door open so that more sounds might get in.

So I stepped out into the city.

It was frightening to be out among the passing of so many vehicles. Why would the vehicles not come after me? But I saw there was a main way, and then, going down the hill, a line of vehicles that had come to rest, and then, where we were standing, a line where no vehicle travelled and that here you might walk. This was different from the mountain, where everything went wherever it chose, and I stood and saw it—that there was an arrangement; that some vast agreement was at work here. This frightened me. How could something so big have been there and I didn't know about it? I looked at Henry, large on the pathway, and he looked right back at me—he knew, as did all the men and woman who were passing now very close about us. Henry stood beside me, with his belly pressing on my elbow. We just stood there, on the pavement, in the city, for a long time and at every moment the feeling grew in me that everyone in the whole world knew everything that I did not.

He leaned down and said, 'Okay, Mr Dog, let's go walkabout.'

We headed downhill and everywhere there were people. We were looking at them and none of them were looking at us. They seemed to know about us already and went around us. We walked down between the buildings on the part of the road that was made for walking. Henry was guiding me so that I was in front of him, with his hand sometimes on my shoulder. I felt the city coming towards my face, like a wind. Now on our left side there was a building where people were cooking and I stopped. I couldn't understand what was happening in all the other buildings but this smelled like the I Fry burger bar. 'Burger King,' said Henry. 'Whatever you say, Mr Dog.'

I knew what a king was but in Henry's words there was more, I knew, of the thing that I couldn't understand. When we were inside it, the Burger King wasn't like our place because the light was dim and the opening at the front was small and so all the smells, of the cooking and of the people, stayed inside. And something hurt my eyes. There was something painful in the air and I began coughing; and so Henry turned us around and returned us to the light.

At the edge of the walking strip—the footpath—was a wooden seat which had three people sitting upon it. I saw that this might be done; that nearby another seat had been placed, I led us there and, following their example, sat down. Henry let me do this. After a moment he sat down beside me.

Before us was the line where the vehicles were all standing, with one vehicle placed directly before us, black and polished, and in the curved black surface of its flank I saw myself, face long and worried.

And, beside me, Henry, long and strange.

Henry which was the only thing that could be counted upon. I look back now and see the boy I was, with dust in his head, with open spaces wide in there, with the crying of high birds, the sound of horses' hooves echoing along a canyon trail, and I remember Henry Stroud and the way he cared for me. I am back now on the mountain but the spaces are gone. Now, the trucks on the great highway are loaded with knowledge which every day passes back and forth before my eyes and somehow that knowledge is a threat. When I dwell on those trucks I begin to frown, and so I direct my thoughts elsewhere. But every day there are more of them. Every day the wires of the pylons sing louder. Now when I see an airplane go over I believe what I am seeing, and perhaps I cower. My father had told me that these were angels.

I see that my father tried to tell me, to teach me and to make me ready to learn. But what I see now is that the task was beyond him. That the world beyond the mountain was perhaps as great a trouble to him as it is to me. Here, when you sweep up a handful of red dirt and let it trickle, your thoughts are filled with the passing of days, each one a speck, and your hand is pleased by the dry running. Such thoughts are comforting and easy to live with. The days like specks of dust, the stars like years, and there are plenty more where they came from. The dirty wind will always play round your ears and lift your hat, will always bowl the tumbleweeds. The hooves of the horses will always ring on the stone of the canyon floor. But it ain't so.

Part Two

Chapter Six

When I was eighteen I turned from the city and the evil that had been done there to me, and rode State Highway One down the throat of the island. The city had spat me out; I had been tossed onto the beach where the dead things are rolled back and forth by each passing wave, where the colour is washed out of them. A wave hit me in the face, I picked myself up—within ten minutes I was gone. This time as I travelled I had a vehicle under me that shifted at my command and, as long as I moved swiftly enough to stay ahead of its owner, I had no need of anyone in the world save the boys who poured petrol.

I had learned a little in the city. A little; perhaps too much. I look back now and this is my surmise. Too much and not enough. But when the time came I saw the highway sign and knew it for what it was. Within ten minutes the white line which is the blood of the blacktop showing through its skin was the thread I was following and my tyres were singing.

There was a dashboard radio and, with the wind in my face, I punched in new stations until I found the old songs that been my solace at the burger bar of Henry Stroud. I had him singing along with me as I drove, the kindest man my eyes ever looked upon and, as I followed the blacktop he travelled along, a ghost rider in my sky. Ghostly too was the dog Blackie, head out the window and yelping, and the ragged pack of street dogs who at my dirty heels had followed him. Also travelling was the girl Spoons, whose eyes looked steadily back at me each time I glanced at the mirror, which was not often. Ghosts all and yet always with me; running with me; south.

How forlorn the little settlements looked as the strip of blacktop took me speeding down through them, their buildings huddled together and their men turned away, as though afraid of what might pass before their eyes. How can you live beside a flowing river and resist the urge to plunge? But I have never been in such places and what do I know?

And so I was delivered into those long-remembered lands by the windscreen of the vehicle, where, as though it was the screen of a movie, the mountain suddenly appeared. I came over the crest of a hill and there it stood, so familiar to my heart that I concentrated on nothing else and thus came close to running off the road. The white lines contained me, and saved me. For the first time that afternoon I lifted my foot, as though at last I had something in front of me that I cared to advance carefully upon; the motor ran down.

Into the late sun I drove, slower now, and there were colours so promising everywhere that I had to squint to make sure I was not fooled. But at last I was certain. It was not the colours of sunset I was seeing but the lands themselves, which were red. At once I allowed the white needle of the speed dial to fall to zero. I turned the vehicle around, pointed it back towards its home, then left it in a roadside picnic area in a covering halo of bushes. I took to my feet.

As I walked, the ghosts sang to me. They called me back. But my mountain was before me and I was going to it.

Going home.

The lands were growing dark; as I walked the red was everywhere being filled with black. I stumbled. But kept going; I would have kept going had I been utterly blind. Strange sounds rang in my ears, old gun fights, terrible cries, but I walked through them, ignored them, caring only to see things I had previously known. Then, finally, a late puff of wind, and before it the roll of a tumbleweed. Like a boy I chased it, and fell. My face plunged into the dirt, which went up my nostrils and got into my eyes and my mouth, so that I spat. But happy. The red dirt has always had its own taste, which had been on my tongue—in my pockets, under my nails—since I was born.

With the darkness the cold was coming and I set about, in the last of the light, pulling brush and tumbleweed together to make a place to lie. I had with me a thick coat which was all I had carried back to the lands and now I wrapped myself in it and, beneath a blanket of dry gatherings, finally stretched my bones out upon the only bed I have ever longed for.

The stars looked down.

Those stars that had hung so still on a thousand nights when my Daddy had bedded beside me now spread their old light upon my cold cheek as I lay wrapped in my coat and so alone. If you seek comfort, never turn to the stars. But for the first time in many years they looked like my stars, as though they knew me, and I knew I was home.

Low against the ragged line the lands made the against the sky tufty silhouettes of tussock and sagebrush could be seen. Little critters went about on pattering feet. A hoot owl called.

Inside my shoes my feet were hardened by the night chill to brittle things that might snap. In the grey light of dawn I found a tall cactus to hide my outline while I stood to relieve myself. The cactuses are no landmarks, they rise and fall too often; but I had no need of such things. These lands I had ridden since I could steady a horse and so now I stepped forward, my feet warming as I went; my heart also. In your own lands you know which quarter the wind will blow from.

The horizon was a still line. Stepping between heads of tussock, I came to a little gulch where there had always been a ribbon of moving water and, finding it again, fell to my knees and drank. The taste rang in my mouth like a bell. I splashed my neck, as my Daddy had told me to do, and felt the shiver go down my spine. Then, so as to move more freely, I rolled the coat, though it was still cold, and tied it into a bundle that I could sling across my back. Thus I strode forth.

I was alone in the lands.

They lay about me, cold from the night, and as I stepped I tried to read the lines that were worn into that great dust-strewn face. 'The land looks up under yr chin,' my Daddy always said, 'so be sure and to wash there.' As I stepped my footprints into the dirt I listened to the crunching they made. It was as though every bird, every little crawling thing in its hole heard this sound and tilted its head to listen too. There goes Chester Farlowe, was what the sounds said and this was somehow a troubling thing that brought a watchful aspect to all that my eye fell upon. Yes, every cactus was making a warning sign. Before long I was walking in a crouch, moving low among the brush as though I expected at any moment to be diving into it.

Yet no challenge came and so I moved steadily onwards, following ways that were known to me, though in truth I had always passed here on horseback. I was working east and north, towards an old trail I knew lay there, that would carry me, winding, up the slopes.

In the mid-morning air the mountain stood, shaggy headed against the grey sky.

In a little draw I came upon a cattlebeast mooching among tousle-headed bushes, foraging disconsolately, and I squatted in shelter and watched. It was of some breed not known to me, with a black hide that shone in the light. On its rump the brand had sunk into the matted hairs there and still I knew it for what it was, the S with two verticals, the Barred S as we used to say, the sign of the dollar. The sign of Stronson. We had always run longhorns, that would gore you just for a glance, and to see this runty animal, which even yet had not detected my presence, filled me with a loathing that was like a running poison. I flung a length of fallen branch, hitting it as I had intended on its bony rump, and the thing broke and ran like the bolter it was.

As I climbed I saw more of these poor beasts, all of them mangy and dull eyed. They were stripping the lands. No matter. I would soon drive them out.

It was true that I had it clear in my head where the course of this river was going to run. There was nothing in my belly but hunger but I had no interest in hunger. I would cook for myself and plenty, soon. And seeing these poor beasts had sickened me; I could not have eaten. Up I went, tirelessly up, and with every step the lands fell below me, spreading as though there was no end to them. Well, I knew the lie of that now. The line of the blacktop was no longer a thing that fascinated; I knew where that fascination led. The pylons too, had changed their tune.

I had, when sent by my Daddy to walk abroad, walked by design beneath the pylon wires and felt all the flesh of me begin to tingle as though some promising feather was being drawn near my skin. My every hair sang, and my teeth sang too, and overhead the wires hung in their swaying loops, heavy with messages. They were, I knew, tubes, and along them ran a kind of water that was like flowing lava—when my Daddy had told me this, I saw the red anger that lay inside the mountain, where we had once been, after I had insisted that I had to see. We climbed to the rim and then down inside. The fumes there had choked me and I fell; he carried me out. But not before I had seen the thing which is inside the mountain, inside the world, which is fire. My Daddy had no opinion of these pylons, so he said, but I had never believed him. There was nothing my Daddy had no opinion about. The truth was, they were syphoning away the power of the mountain, and he thought this would be knowledge too terrible for me to bear. But I had my own ideas about those pylons, about the swinging wires. One great day they would come down.

But for now they sighed in the dirty wind and as I listened I understood what the foreign cattlebeast had said to me into the clatter of its escaping hooves, what the water had said as it went its low course. It was in the shape of the mountain which could never change—and yet had changed. There were strangers here.

This knowledge grew to certainty in me as I made my way up the gentle rise of the foothills. The afternoon was fading now, and soon the cold would come. Even I could not climb in the dark and so I looked for a place to bed down. It would be, I knew, a hiding place. Which sickened me, and made the anger build. To be hiding here, where my name was written in the dust—this was shaming.

I found a dry watercourse and gathered first brush for my bedding and then wood, which I lit with matches from the pocket of my coat.

At first it was a low fire, which I bent over, warming my hands. But as the cold gathered and the darkness grew blacker, as the stars came out, and memories of fires shared with my Daddy came flickeringly to me, I began to throw on larger pieces, and to glory in the way that the pillar of flame streaked upwards. This was my home! It will always be my home! I am here by right! My fire shouted these words out and the jumping shadows all around me were like spirits released after a long imprisonment. The watercourse was cupped like a hand and in its hollow I felt as though the land had made a place for me.

I remembered fires shared with my Daddy on this very mountainside, and one great blaze that Henry Stroud built for us on a beach, and dirty little fires squatted over with the girl Spoons in the back seats of abandoned cars and beneath overpasses in drizzly rain when the curling smoke had clung with the tiny beads of damp to her twist of hair. My ghosts, who travelled with me.

The fire rose and inside me the feelings rose also, as I remembered, that I had been done wrong, had been stolen from, and made to pay, and made to work, and never paid, that my Daddy had been torn from me, and also my life on the mountain, which was all I loved and all I had—the fire crackled and the sound was angry talk to me, as though the very elements would speak out my feelings. So I went deeper and deeper into the blaze, ever deeper into the leaping colours, which grew like the hunger twisting in my belly. Thus my head was down and my eyes so flooded by dancing light that it was some time before I grasped that beyond the flames there was standing a figure.

I saw first his boots, tooled and heeled, with cruel spurs. My eyes travelled up the long legs wrapped in the dusty chaps, saw there beside the legs the long barrel of the hefted rifle. Beneath a broad hat stood the coward Stronson, watching down on me, and the flames cast streaks of emotion on his face, loathing and cunning, which, blotchy, swam together in evil communion. His complexion, which ran naturally to freckles, was now a livid assemblage of spots, which danced; his watching eyes were the dancingest spots of all, deep set and cold—I leapt to my feet and, keeping the fire between us, ran headlong into the dark. I fell, twisted to one side—I knew that any moment the rifle would crack, that the small length of spinning lead would fly, humming, like a hornet making an angry line, spinning, spinning, seeking; would smack into my back and explode me open. I scrabbled, crawled, ran on. My face was torn by the long spines of a cactus which blocked my path, but I had no time to care for that, I could hear his boots crunching behind me, hear the action of his rifle as he worked the bolt.

Or so I thought. In fact the crack never came. There was no bullet, or even a footfall—that had all been, I realised, in my head. I was crouched now behind a low bush and all I could hear was my heart, which was thunderous. When cautiously I glimpsed from behind its branches I saw the flames, quite distant now, and then his tall shape, watching from the shadows beneath his hat. He was listening for me, was judging where to direct his fire—but no. He stood and, though I was too far away to see his eyes, I knew that they were trying to see me. But no. Instead he called.

His voice was full of honey, full of remorse and warmth. Into the night he called my name, 'Chester,' and his voice was full of the sing-song that the girl Spoons had called to me with, 'Chester, Chester,' full of emotion and regretful knowledge. But I knew this for the treachery that it was and, crawling low on my belly, I crept away from him, and out into the silence of the cold dark of the mountain's foothills.

In my haste I had left my coat, which had been my soft seat in the dust by the fire, also my leather jerkin, which I had shed as the flames went to my bones, and now the cold began to come for me as though I was a thing that it might have and own. On my skin the sweat was drying beneath its cake of dust, like a plaster cast, and blood dribbled from the cuts made by the spines of the cactus.

But I had no pause to dwell on these things. Behind me, Stronson was coming, slow, ear turned, and so I must go on, on my belly and away from the light. Once a rattler spoke warningly with his shaker of bones and I twisted away. Once my hand went deep into a thick pile of dung left by a cattlebeast. None of this mattered. True, I was a shivering length of fear; I was on my belly and would go lower if I had to—I would burrow right into the dirt. But at the heart of the fear a red inch of anger—of hate—was twisting like a blind worm. Looking for a way out into the world.

Finally I had crawled far enough and, finding a dense thicket, crawled inside, where I waited. The night was thickly dark. My hand was cupped behind my ear, listening keenly. I stopped my breathing. But still I was the loudest thing. From inside me came a terrible churning. Out of the lands, there was no sound. Peering from behind the brush, I could make the darkness take tall shapes—There he is! He is raising his rifle!—but these were only the shadows of my mind. Above, the stars watched coldly down. What did you expect, they said, that he cut down your father so that he could ride away? He always wanted these lands. What did you expect, that you would just walk in and take back your home?

But that was not what I had expected. I had come to get my guns.

I passed the night within the thicket. I say within, but in truth the shelter was thin. The cold had formed about me like a shroud, setting hard. I drew up my limbs, wrapped myself tight. There was a cinder at the centre of me that I had to keep alive. Behind me, inside the mountain, I knew that there was red fire, and I set my mind to keep a picture of that before me, red and fiery, something to draw heat from. Well, it served. When the dawn came I was still alive.

Slowly I unfolded.

The lands lay about, patchy in the first light, as though pools of water had seeped to the surface. Nothing moved. I made my guess about which quarter my fire might have been in and studied the grey air for any wisp of smoke. Of course I saw many wisps, but then, hungry, sleepless, every shadow was alive for me, every shape was a picture. I thought I saw Stronson twenty times. I thought I saw my ghosts, come to comfort me. But no. Finally I could stay still no longer and began, in painful slowness, to retrace my steps.

This was not difficult. There in the dust was a long, flat line where my belly had twisted. There were torn branches and, on the flat table of a stone, two red spots where I had bled—my hand went to my cheek and found something thick and matted.

As I came close to the little draw where my fire had been I went more slowly and tried to move with stealth. How loud I suddenly was. Then, from bushes ahead, a jackrabbit broke, and while I would dearly liked to have chased him I took comfort from the fact that if the critters were surprised by me then surely I was the only man about. And so I went closer and looked down upon my fire.

No one.

Ah—and my coat and jerkin! Just as I had left them.

I was about to dive for them, but suddenly held myself. It would be his cruel trick, I thought, to let me believe I was alone. Me so fearsome—no guns, no breakfast, shivering and dishevelled; oh yes, this you would need to gain further advantage over, if you were a coward, a back-shooter. But in the brush little birds were singing. To one side I saw a tortoise come staggering from beneath a tilted rock and, waiting until he was clear, I plunged and grasped him and turned him on his back. It was painful to see the way his legs wriggled in the air; and to know that for all his wriggling he was soon going to be dead. But I could not afford to dwell upon this, as there were shapes which marked the dust and I should go and study them.

Like a pale bird of thought, I look down now on the fellow I was then, so young and so full of headlong impulses and ghosts and ignorance. I try to imagine how what followed could have been averted. I can't see it. Everything he did I would, had I been him, have done; if I had known what he knew—if I had not known what he did not know. We make the best of what we have and thus are formed. And in the years that follow we must choose: shall we plunge on, headlong, living always in the midst of being formed? Or have we reached that day when we know all that we are going to know, and say, Now I will live with it.

The fire was no more than charred sticks though I knew at a glance that I could blow life back into it. But that would have run a flag up into the clear morning sky. I needed heat; I was hunched over by the cold, and there to hand was fire, my coat and jerkin. But still I held back, fighting, clenching my teeth and making myself—my heart—even colder. I stood and looked hard about until I was sure I had seen all that could be seen.

Stronson's pointed boots had not moved very far. Their tracks took him down to the fire, where he had squatted. There was a mark where the butt of his rifle had rested. He'd twisted, looking about. Then, a departing line of tracks took him away into the north—I guessed that if I went that way I would find the hooves of his horse. But he had left something. There in the dust were the marks made by his finger. Writing—after a long struggle I made out the first word, which was my name. The wind had blown the letters. But that was not my struggle. At that time I could not read.

With the lands spread wide open around me, and the morning light so clear, I squatted in the dust and found a new reason to hate Stronson. That his killer's finger had written my name—I remembered now him calling it into the night, sweet and beckoning, and red flooded my eyes. I would kill him.

Though I hated it that he could write and I could not read, his message, whatever it was, had no meaning for me. I would kill him. I threw the jerkin onto my back, swung the coat up and wrapped myself. Then I turned and, seizing the turtle, cracked its back open and drank its warm blood. Chin dribbling, I started up the mountain.

As I climbed, the lands began to stretch before my eye. Whenever there was a little cover, I would stand and survey the lined face spread below me. Weathered and marked and always watching. 'You better had wash under your chin,' my Daddy had said, and my hand went there. I was no doubt filthy. My cheek was stiff with blood. But the crisp air of that mountainside was in my head like a cooling stream. I ran my eye along the length of the blacktop, I traced the swaying arc of the pylon wires. I knew clearly what I would do.

In a tableland which jutted from the mountain's side was the place and when I was there the feelings which came to me were so strong that I had to sink to my knees. My Daddy's bones were here, beneath the dust and rock, and, though there was no marker, no sign, they would always be here. I knelt and I missed him. My ghosts were about me and I wanted to say, Henry Stroud, this is my father. Spoons, this is the man. Daddy, these people here are my friends. But I was alone, and they all three of them were gone from me.

It was terrible hard digging with my hands but I did not mind. My fingers worked; with a small stick I pecked at stones which had settled firm in the six years since I had been gone. When finally I saw the glint of metal, the sun was falling from the sky and the cold shadow of the mountain was swinging towards me. But my task was nearly done.

I strapped the guns to my hips. The belt was too long and I adjusted it so that it hugged me. The rawhide threads I tied round my thighs; and I stood. Then I came into my anger. It bit into me. I was shaken by the venom as it flooded through me; I knew that there was no turning back. A man now, I buckled the guns onto my hips and stood with my face to the gritty wind, and the red lands were red and the blue sky was red and the black highway was red behind the curtain of blood which was flowing down over the world.

Six years in the earth had rotted holes in my old coat, which was anyway now too small for me, but I took it and, in the last of the light, descended. It would, I knew, be a little warmer lower down. I had the lariat across my back and, across my face, the white-spotted bandana that I had worn so long ago. My boy's chaps were short but still warmed my legs and as I went my spurs jingled, which was a song that I knew.

This time my fire was smaller, and better hidden, and this time I had a great rock at my back so that he could not come up behind me. I planned a route that I would run, which would quickly lead to a good ambush place. By the light of the flames I roasted turtle pieces on a stick and fed myself. These were no cheeseburgers but, in my anger, cheeseburgers were not what I wanted. I felt as though I had been filled with the smoke from one of Spoons' damp cigarettes, that the smoke in there had curdled and thickened my head. Everything that stoked my rage was all that I wanted, and I sat and felt myself becoming a murderer.

But the smell of the lands was stronger.

Yes, as the fire fell, I stretched myself beside it, and spread the boy's coat, tattered and holed, over me. But I was inside my good coat, and, with the jerkin, I was as warm as a gopher in a hole. In my right hand I clutched a gun and it was as heavy as intent. But as I lay there, with the fire going down, and the great shoulder of the mountain behind me, and the stars coming out, I felt my rage ebb away. If I thought of Stronson's name I could bring it back, and I did this, feeling the kick and surge of it go through me. But there was no need. Stronson would keep. And so I lay in the shelter of the rock, under a covering of brush, with the sweet smell of the land riding over all that was in me, and allowed sweeter thoughts to come to me.

I thought of Henry Stroud, how he would have liked this place. True, there was no ocean in which to fish, but the colour of the lands, so red and rich, would have pleased him. I heard him saying, 'So, Mr Dog,' and gazing about as though he was master, too, of all this. I saw his great rolling eye, his scarred head, going over the lands, and as he went his radio would be playing. I knew the song. I had heard it singing in his comfortable room and now as I lay I sang it to myself.

Hear the cattle calling
Hear the clopping of the horse
Watch the river running
In its deep and silent course

See the stars come brightly
Cast their glimmer on the lands
Reach out
And you've got home
Within your hands.

I needed a horse and I could not immediately see how I might have one.

I stayed in the small camp I had made beneath the rock for three days, making myself once more into a thing of these lands. Inside my head, the sounds of Auckland city gradually faded. Now the sound I heard loudest was the wind, which was always whispering. Ear cocked, I heard cattle moving far out on the edge of my hearing. I heard the distant shouts of cowhands and, deep, the thud of horse's hooves. These sounds brought pictures to me and, squatting, I would stare at the hole in the air in front of me and study them.

I heard the private sounds of the critters as they went about their lives. I watched an eagle go gliding slow to a high nest on tipping wings.

I heard the song that said the wind was called Maria.

Six years had passed and I had grown out of my boyhood coat. I had lost everything in the world that I had loved. But I had gained these songs, which came and went inside my head as though they each one had something to tell me. The song that said there was a bad moon rising. That said I went down, down, down, in a burning ring of fire. That said that only the lonely know the way I feel tonight. These songs had been on Mr Stroud's radio.

And sometimes the pictures that came to me were of him; of me on my high chair, and the burger bar humming, and him back in the comfortable room, under his low light, warming his feet on the dog Blackie and the singing of the radio. It was strange: when I was there the songs made me think of my Daddy and our life on the lands; and now I was home on the lands the songs made me think of Henry Stroud.

But mostly the pictures were of the girl called Spoons. She had sang these songs. 'They're oldies,' she would say, 'you like mouldy oldies, Chester.' Her mother had liked these songs, she said, and she'd heard them when she was growing up, and knew all the words. In the back of old cars we would sit, with the rain falling down, and she would kneel on the upholstery and sing them right into my face.

Her skin was covered in pimples. There were pimples on her forehead and on her cheeks and on her neck and sometimes, when she got into a mood, she would sit in front of a mirror and squeeze until there was blood. 'You wanna do one, Chester?' she would say, and then laugh, ha, ha, ha. But she hated them. When she was singing she would say, 'Look in my eyes, cowboy,' and if my eyes wandered to her face she would take my chin in her hand and twist it until I did. So I would be looking right in there, right into those dark eyes of hers, brown as swamp water, with her hand holding my chin, harshly at first, and then just staying there, holding me, her fingers stroking while she sang to me. *Feel so sad, I've got a worried mind.*

She knew all the words and she would sing slowly, and make her eyes swell when she said certain things, *my baby just cares for me,* and then bring her eyelids down, slowly, *an' livin' is easy,* and then her eyes would pop open, *he jus' keeps rollin' along,* to see if she still had me. Which she did. Her eyes had me, and her hand on my chin had me, and also her other hand, which would slowly, very, very slowly, be undoing the buttons of my trousers.

At night on the lands I would sit over my fire, remembering

how she sang those songs to me and my Daddy's words would come floating back on the wind. 'The day will come,' he would say, 'when you look at the mountain and think of her. You will see her in the way your horse walks, and you will smell her in the smell of your lariat, and you will look out over the lands and not see anything but her, everywhere you look and nowhere that can be seen.' He had told me that this would happen and now it was happening and I didn't have him here to tell me what to do about it.

But the songs would come into my head and I would remember. In the middle of an island, in the middle of an ocean. She would finally run out of buttons and her eyes would blink, once, as though she was surprised. She would shake her head so that her dark hair moved. At first she would toss it so as to settle it into a new place and then she would move it again, just a little, stir it so that it said something to me. Far, far away on my island of dreams, she would sing, and she would take me in her hand and all the time she had hold of my chin so that I couldn't see. The air was all fuggy and damp, it was always raining when Spoons and I were in the cars, otherwise we'd be outside, and sometimes I would look at the blue and pray for rain—not a cloud in the sky. She wouldn't let me touch her. 'You keep your filthy hands to yourself,' she'd say. 'Your cowboy hands, Chester. Where's your hat, cowboy? Where's your guns? Is this your gun? Is it gunna go off, Chester?' She liked to talk as though she was mean and evil. But I knew mean and evil and Spoons was as soft as a fall of snow. 'If it goes off I'm outa here, Chester, I'm gunna be hittin' the trail. Want me to hit the trail, Chester?' But she was looking right into my eyes when she said this and she was singing to me—Goldfingers, she's the girl with the spider's touch—and I knew that everything my Daddy had said was true, if only I could remember it. 'I like to torture you, Chester,' she would say, regretfully, and shake her head so that her hair, filled with all the little droplets of rain, would move on her shoulders.

In the cars we would smoke and also when we were outside, at the beach or maybe in Myers Park. The smoke filled you up, filled your belly, which was a good thing since a lot of the time we were eating air. All the cheeseburgers that Mr Stroud had put on me fell away. But I didn't care. I didn't look for food. That wasn't what I was thinking about.

In Myers Park there were palm trees and Spoons said, 'It's an oasis, Chester.' The park sloped in at the sides, and at the bottom there was a gravel path which went through and we would swing on the swings and watch everyone that went along the path. Spoons would tell me about them. 'He's got a wife that's too much for him and he's going off in his lunchtime to look at toy trains,' she'd say. 'He's a train man. Chuff, chuff, chuff, train man.' And she would pass me the smoke.

I would just have a little draw on it so as not break out choking, though Spoons would say, 'Choking's good. Choking draws the smoke right down into your lungs—gets you higher.' She would be swinging like crazy when she said these things and I would be watching her and thinking that on the upswing she was going to fly right off and figuring how I could run and catch her. But I couldn't run. I could only walk, and slowly at that. My legs were filled with heavy smoke and everything was worth studying. I liked the green of the grass in Myers Park. I would see how the colour of it was so strong that it made a sound. I would bring my swing down to the bottom and just sit, listening to the sound of the green of the grass, which went off in every direction. Spoons would be swinging giant swings beside me and the sound of that was like a huge roaring.

Then she slowed and came down beside me and said, 'Is you mah baby, cowboy?'

'Sure am, darlin'.' She taught me to say this.

Sometimes someone would go past and she would say, 'There goes pussy pants.' Or, 'There goes a briefcase taking its man for a walk.' Then she'd look at me to see if I understood.

But sometimes she'd say, 'You wanna *be* mah baby?' And this I did understand. At one side of Myers Park where it sloped up towards some buildings there were trees. You couldn't sleep there, because at night the police would come with torches—she told me that. But in the day it was shady and, if you went right up against the brick wall of the park, private. You could hear cars going past, but far away. If we had been smoking, everything was far away. At the top of the brick wall was a fence and, set back from the fence, the buildings, where people lived. But they never came and looked down into the park.

Spoons had a spot she liked to sit in, with her back against a tree, with, beside her, a place for me, so that we could kiss. It was like a house under the trees, like a room, with leaves above us, and down in front, and just little specks of light coming through. The smoke made me think about how many leaves there might be. Down in front was a grassy slope of green and I liked the angle of this slope. We kissed. I had never done any kissing—'Not even a single kiss?' said Spoons, and I had to tell her. Well, she soon showed me.

Sometimes people walked on the gravel down on the path and their crunching feet could be heard. But that was just a faraway sound among faraway sounds, that were just part of the world going on, outside. We were there, kissing, and I just wanted to stay inside that place for as long as she would let me. Long, long kisses and then looking into her eyes. The light was dim in under the trees but I could see Spoons in her eyes, the way you can see the whole world inside the eye of a horse when you're right up close, I could see the whole world of Spoons inside there. She let me stroke her cheek and touch her hair. She would say, 'You really love me, don't you, Chester.' She said it so full of feeling.

And I would say, 'I dunno, baby. Plenty of fish in the sea.'

If I didn't say that she would get a piece of my cheek and pinch it. So I said it. And she would say, 'I'm gonna break your heart, cowboy.'

'You a devil woman, Spoons. You a terrible heartbreaker.' If I said this right she would take my head in her hands and give it a tiny shake, and grin. Then her mouth would come close to mine and we would kiss.

Inside my head there was the huge rushing sound.

And she would say, 'You wanna *be* my baby, baby?'

While I waited she would unto the buttons of her shirt. She did it so slowly. My eyes would study her fingers. Sometimes her finger would go round and round a button. 'Is it fascinatin', baby?' she would ask. But this was gentle. And it *was* fascinating, and she thought so too. She would put my head inside her shirt and all the time I was there she was so gentle, which was a thing I had never known could be extended. That closeness could be extended. That it could go on, so long that it was a thing that you were inside, that you were inside of and staying inside of. She would stroke my head and put her fingers in my hair, and talk to me. She would whisper, as though someone might hear. But there was no one.

Sometimes she would do up the top button so that I was

caught in there. I didn't mind. She would whisper down into my ear. She would say, 'And then your old horse would go clip-cloppin' along through the lonesome canyon and you would be ridin' slow, with buzzards flyin' and eagles flyin', just little specks high over head, goin' ever which way, and then in the distance you would see that the goldarn injuns was sendin' up them smoke signals again.' And she'd prod me so I would make a murmur of assent. Sometimes she'd actually make me break off and speak. But that was just her wanting to inflict a little torture and I didn't mind. Sometimes she'd tell me that squads of policemen were crawling towards us and any minute would crack our heads. But what she most liked talking about was my life. She'd say, 'And then your old horse would come down the mountainside on the homeward trail, and you'd let the reins go slack in your hands, because that ol' horse knows where to go, and you'd look about you, over the lands, and see how in the faraway distance there was a fire. An' that fire meant that your Daddy was home aheada you and was cookin' for you and that soon you'd be gettin' yo' vittles. An' all around the lands looked like some wonderful dustman had been wanderin' over them, spreadin' his dust, and it was all so smooth, like sand, 'cept it wasn't sand, it was red and had little ridges in it, made by the wind, where the gila monsters ran, where all them gophers and coyotes ran, and the rattlers an', what, the water moccasin snakes went slidin' an' the tumbleweeds kept rollin' along. Just the clip-clopping of that old horse and the little jingle from your spurs, an' your hat makin' a band of sweat round your brow. Cactuses standin' up like telegraph poles, like them signals they have on the railway with arms out and pointin' which way to go. How them horse hooves do echo, Chester.'

'Yes, darling.'

'Yes, darling Spoons whom you love like a flower loves the spring.'

'Yes, darling.'

'Yes, darling Spoons whom you love like a schoolboy loves his pie.'

'Yes, darling.'

'River deep and mountain high, Chester. River deep and mountain high.' Which I knew was a song.

Then she would stroke my head and sing the song that I liked best.

> *Way out here they've got a name*
> *For rain and wind and fire.*
> *The rain is Tess*
> *The fire's Joe*
> *And they call the wind Maria.*

So for three days I sat over my fire learning myself back into the lands and everywhere I looked I saw her and every time I listened I heard her voice. But she wasn't there and would never be there and the longer I sat the better I knew that I could not sit, that I would have to move.

And for that I needed a horse.

Chapter Seven

In the distance I had been hearing sounds of cattle. The thud of hooves on dirt, bellowing—on the wind called Maria these sounds came and I knew that somewhere in the western distance there was a big herd. Cowboys yelling and, at dusk, the call of a single beast that had lost its calf.

An idea came into my mind and I commenced to walk.

To the west lay lands that were strange to me. My Daddy had, most years, run our herd towards the north where the feed was not so good and so we were pretty much left to our own devising. Though we had the best water, and when the rains were thin sometimes the westlanders would bring their herds up our way. My Daddy allowed this. Our herd was pure longhorn and you could tell at a lariat's length which beast was ours. Those times were full of watching and I knew he was relieved when the rains came and we once again were alone in our dusty, wind-scoured homelands.

We had hunted, though, in the west, for turkey and once for a wolf which was hiding out there but killing among our beasts. Now as I made my way through the broken lands that lay at the limit of where we usually did our droving I did see turkey feathers and once I heard a gobble in among some brush. But I had resolved not to fire my guns and so I kept walking, and ate lizards and gopher snakes. Which you have to be hungry for. But I was.

My Daddy always said, an army marches on its belly, which was something he had heard and, like so many things he told me, I only began to get the sense of what this might mean when he was no longer with me. My belly marched me through the broken lands; the eye inside my stomach said, cain't see much to be ingesting here. I kept going. Being hungry makes you see everything. The stomach eye, sure, which, as Spoons said, could spot a promising rubbish tin at five hundred yards. But up in your head the eyes there seem to catch the world as though everything in it has been cut from paper, so that the outlines of all you see are sharp and have a black glow at the edge. High on either side of me now mesas were rising, in strange layered shapes that sometimes looked like piles of flapjacks. They were cut about by the wind and some were so high and narrow that if you waited just a minute they were sure to fall. But I had never seen this happen and my Daddy neither. 'Along here's one looks like the head of Moses,' he told me one time, 'and he's been astandin' there since he managed to put down them tablets, and he'll be here when you and I an' all your littl'uns are just dust in the breeze, amen.' We were on horseback then and Moses went past at a steady clip. But now as I placed one boot after another my hungry eyes went over his stone face, as high as a cliff, and he seemed to ask what I was doing there. So I looked away. Whenever I got to thinking, I was soon filled with feelings that weakened me—anger, loneliness—and so I just looked at the sky, where high birds were circling, and studied the shapes of things, the cloud shapes and the broken line of the land against them, and kept my boots moving.

As night fell on the fourth day out I knew from the sounds that I would arrive among the cattle in the morning and so I bedded down in the knowledge that soon I would again be among men and having once again to explain myself.

I lay in the flickering light of my small fire and tried not to think. Above me the head of a butte made great shapes in the night. The stars beyond it were, now that I had no need of comfort, quite content to shine warmly on me. I was well wrapped in my big coat, with the old boy's one on top and my boots towards the flames. It is good to sleep on the land. It doesn't bounce under you, it doesn't shift to conform to you. The land is hard. But it is not hollow. Even when the ground is cold you know that far below old things are slowly moving. Spoons once took me to a place called an IMAX where there were, on a wall, pictures of the grinding and bubbling and creeping that, underground, goes on every day. Sleeping out, it's like being on the back of a huge thing that is alive—on the back of an elephant, maybe, except the elephant is as big as the world.

Not when you're in the city, of course.

A coyote barked in the distance, and from far away there was an answering call. A long cloud came across the stars. The top of my head was cold, but very clear. I would walk early and, when I was sure of arriving, shoot three turkeys so as to arrive with something for dinner and also so that the shots would let them know I was coming. It was possible they would send a spare man to look me over. But that would be a bad sign, as I hoped they had no such spare man and would welcome me.

Then we would see what we would see.

Now a wolf called and, along with every man for thirty miles, I stilled myself and listened out for a response. Nothing, and more nothing. Then, from the west, came a high, high wo-wo-woo which I knew was a cowboy, laying in his bedding and making his best call. The wolf was not fooled. But fools were lying thickly on the ground and soon the night was thick with cowboy wolves all singing their best timberwolf songs. Then a cow called and in the bell of its note I heard the question that every cowboy fears: do I have to run? That was the end of the wolf calling.

Then, high above, something dark and immense passed across the pattern of the stars.

In the morning I kicked over my fire and set off to find a fresh. I took some care with my washing. The blood on my cheek was old now and I rubbed a good deal of it away, though there were still three long scratches. Before screwing my hat into place I slicked down my hair.

After which I strode out in search of my turkeys.

It had been six years since I had actually fired a gun and when finally a gobbler presented himself I got excited and squeezed too soon. High—the bullet passed over his head, hit a rock, went whizzing away. The bird ran fatly, slam into his brother, then his other brother, the noise was terrible—I took a bead and, bang, in a cloud of feathers he went down.

Then I had to figure: should I pluck him? That would cheer up the cook, but then there would be flies. On the other hand, it would be nice not to heft all those feathers. In the end I planned to delay the plucking and walk a bit closer, then decide. In my head the shots were still echoing. It was as though I had shouted, I am here. Little rocks tumbled down cliff faces, every bird was silent. To call everyone to look at you, that is not the right way to live on the lands. I tried to measure how far it might be to where the herd was grazing. Two hours' walk, maybe. But if I was carrying three turkeys? Three hours.

The sun was climbing and I made myself set off. I had the boy's coat over one shoulder so that the turkey blood could drip without harm and so I walked. It was hot and sweat streaked me. Dust swam in my face. But this is how it is on the lands. If you have a horse, well, mostly you're above the grit which sweeps along at ground level. On foot, the landscape goes past so slowly that it seems to be still. But when you look back all you can see is that things have changed.

In a little draw I heard gobbling and went to do the necessary. This time it took only one bullet each—those turkeys can run, if only they can once decide to do it—and then I set to plucking.

As I came up on the herd I felt my blood rising. There is nothing like a herd of cattle for stirring up the dust and the air was full of it, a soft greyness making a billow you could see for miles. Occasionally a shout would echo off the sides of the canyon through which they were travelling and I knew that shortly I would again be in the company of men. I sat myself upon a rock and pulled the last of the turkey feathers. Then I walked on.

Now I could smell the herd, which was such a familiar smell to me that despite myself I smiled. There was a dog who came running out on his own to find me. He circled, yipping, and then was called away by a cry. I knew it would not be long now, and indeed only some minutes had passed when a lone horseman came trotting out of the haze. This I figured would be the bossman.

He pulled his horse up short about three strides from me and gazed around at the horizon as though there were things of great interest there. Then he spoke down. 'Lemme see,' he said, still addressing the horizon, 'you've got no ride, no bedroll, nothin' but your boots and a cupla long furrows in your cheek that some crazy girl made—am I right? Not a dime anywheres about your person but you're the handiest little cowpoke this side of the singin' river—speakin' of which you smell like a polecat. An' you walked out here just to stretch your lonely legs.'

Now he did turn his gaze upon me and I saw that he was in fact a man kindly disposed towards the world, who talked tough so as to not be a pushover. 'Okay, then. Okay. What about you take them birds to ol' Chowder back there an' ask him how you can avoid bein' a hindrance. An' then we'll see.'

He turned his animal. Then he looked back over his shoulder. 'Bin in the city?'

I nodded.

'Takes everythin' from ya, donit. You can ride, cain't you?'

I nodded again.

'Do you speak?'

'Yes, sir.'

'What's your name?'

I hadn't anticipated this question. 'Dog,' I said.

He nodded sagely. 'Dog. Okay. Okay, Mr Dog. You can call me Lennox.'

I saw he was preparing to go and I spoke quickly. 'Sir, who is the owner of these cattlebeasts?'

'The brand is on the rump, son. Sign o' the dollar. Mr Stronson is the man hereabouts—okay with you?'

'Okay with me,' I said. And he rode away.

As I watched his horse kick up the dust I wondered if my face had spoken when Stronson's name had hit the air. A trailboss like Lennox can spot a missing nail in a horseshoe at ten thousand paces. If he had any idea who I was he had not shown it. But who would have suspected that I would be there, when six long years had passed?

I circled round the herd until, upwind, I saw the

chuckwagon with, on its wooden steps, a bareheaded man peeling potatoes into a pail of water. I looked down at my birds. They were dripping steadily and bumped against my knee at every second stride, and they were terrible heavy. But that meant they were fat.

Now as I came up close I saw that the bareheaded man had been watching me and all once his gaze swung up to meet mine. And I had a terrible shock and wanted to run: I knew this man. Or had at least seen him before, as he was distinctive looking—very thin, with a tall thin head that looked as though it was all bone and tight-stretched skin. He had once come to our sleepout to ask my Daddy for work. Daddy said we didn't run a work-offerin' kind of operation but would he care to spend the night, seein' as how he'd rode so far, from the city. And so this elongated man had folded himself into a shape by our fire, and talked, and told us about things he had seen, which, after he was gone, gave me and Daddy conversational subjects for some months.

But I couldn't run and so I stood, head down a little so that maybe my hat would hide my eyes, and held out my birds. The cook took me in very slowly, as though he might be forced to give an accounting of me. 'Mr Chowder, sir,' I said, 'Mr Lennox said I orta ask you how not to be a hindrance.'

The thin-faced man continued to study me as though he was searching for something I might have hidden. 'He always says to say that,' said the man finally, 'if he thinks it likely you'll be completely without a use. It's a kind of code between us.' My turkeys dripped steadily. 'Okay, Master Chester,' he said. 'Sling your birds on the tailgate and come and finish these here.' And he dropped a half-peeled potato into the pail.

'They call me Dog, sir,' I said.

'Dog, is it. That's a fine name, Master Chester; anyone

who had a choice would definitely pick out the name of Dog for themselves, yes sir.' He had a small mouth and when he talked he only allowed it to open a little, as though he wanted to make sure that nothing escaped unless he planned it. 'Now is Dog the first name you have or the aftername?'

'It's the only name I have, sir.'

'So it's Mr Dog?'

'Yes, sir.'

'Very good, Mr Dog. Very good. It will be a pleasure to have someone to call out *Hey Mr Dog* to when there's nothin' else to do with the day.' His grey eyes were large in his thin face and there was a sense that they drew fiercely from all they fell upon, and held it—and yet he was as thin as though there was nothing inside. But there was. There was memory in there, which, though small, can contain the whole world, everything ever seen or heard of. In there he knew he had seen me before—not only seen me, but where he had seen me, and what my name was. As I laid my birds on the flat tailgate of his wagon I shivered a little.

And yet. That little mouth that was so small and tight; that mouth was a gate that many things would not be allowed to pass. He was thin, this man, like a running rail that you sat on at the corral; like a skinny tree standing all alone in the hot sun. Part of the landscape, and liked it that way: he might keep his little mouth shut.

No one made more than a grunt when, that night, seated round the steady fire, Lennox told them that my name was Dog, Mr Dog, and that I had walked up out of the land with these here birds that we were presently eatin'. There were five cowboys and a cowgirl. I had never seen a cowgirl before, or even heard of such a thing, but here she was, a living example, sitting on a flat stone like everyone else and concentrating on downing on her chow. Her name was Miss Peet and nothing special was made of her, so I tried to keep my eyes to myself. There were two Mexicans who did manage to look once at me as they grunted, a small man called Daniels, a scar-faced man named Henley; then Mr Lennox said, 'And this is the Sultation Kid. Sultation.' And stepped back. Now this last named of the cowboys set down his plate, stepped through the fire and came to stand over me. With a forefinger he lifted his hat. He tilted his head on his neck and stared down at me with one large yellow eye. Over the other he wore a black patch. 'I see ya got a man's guns there, son,' he said. 'Lemme see.' It was hard to resist that one eye, cocked at you like a bird, so I slipped one of Daddy's pistols from its holster and, turning it butt-first, passed it up to him. He had large hands and he hefted the gun as though it might be necessary to shake a bullet into the chamber. Then, suddenly, he swung it to the skies and fired off three shots up at triangulated stars. 'Going high and to the right,' he said dismissively. He lifted the barrel to his lips, blew in case there might have been a puff of smoke, then pointed the weapon at me. Looking up, I saw the yellow moon behind his head. I was still reeling from the sound of the shots and now as well as the moon I saw his large round eye and then, closer, the black hole of the barrel. Inside that hole was death but all that roundness was overwhelming and I began to laugh. Laughter spread round the fire and in the flickering light of the flames a change could be seen to come over the features of the one-eyed man. His black eyebrows came together, then it looked as though he might cry. He turned on the heel of one well-tooled boot and flung my gun out into night, where it was clear from the thud that came that it had hit an animal. There was a bellow, the gun clattered against some rock, then: bang—it went off.

Can you really see a bullet in flight? Like a shooting star this one made a line against the heavens. It tore into the black hat of the Sultation Kid, ripping it from his head and tipping it into the fire. The Kid was completely bald, a fact which apparently the hat had concealed from his fellow cowboys ever since he had known them, to judge by their laughter. The Kid swore angrily, grabbed the smouldering hat, tossed it to the ground, then doused it with the only water he had available at that moment.

This event took place directly before the seated Miss Peet, who never once flickered. A hand came up to protect her food from the worst of the splashes.

'Now,' said the man named Henley, 'put it on your head.'

'First put that thing away,' said Miss Peet, 'it's puttin' me off my chow.'

But this was an instruction the Kid had no intention of obeying. He was searching, anyone could see, for a way to regain if not his dignity then at least a sense that he was someone to be reckoned with, and he thought he had found it. His hands went to the back of his smooth, round head, and he flexed his shoulders and gazed up at the stars. He was hung like a horse. Lennox said, 'Now, Kid, we've all seen that cucumber of yours too many times. Attend to your buttons.'

The Kid said, 'The boy ain't seen.'

'He has now,' said Lennox.

'An' he's quakin' in his boots,' said Daniels.

'Son,' said the Kid, 'you ever see anythin' like that?'

'Aw, go fuck a hole in a tree,' said the man named Henley.

Beneath their sombreros, the Mexicans ate steadily.

Now the small man, Daniels, stood slowly and began

fumbling with his trousers. 'Ah nivver showed ya this,' he said. And he displayed himself in a manner similar to the Kid. Now two men were heads back, gazing at the stars.

'Ah reckon it's bigger,' said Henley.

This remark hung in the air.

'What!' said the Kid and his eye swung down.

The Mexicans ate steadily.

'Ahm sorry, Kid,' said the small man. 'I nivver meant for you to know.'

'It is not bigger!' thundered the Kid.

Henley said, 'Try lookin' with ya good eye.'

'Won county fairs in two states,' said the small man modestly.

'Miss Peet,' said Lennox, 'I believe we need an adjudicating word from you.'

'A smoking hole with black hairs round it,' said Miss Peet calmly, not looking up.

The Mexicans ate steadily.

That night as I lay under the stars my head tilted and rocked, as though inside it the events of the evening were sloshing from side to side. I had never before been witness to such behaviour. A woman like Miss Peet was beyond my experience and I struggled to grasp what it was I'd seen. Spoons had at times acted in a vulgar manner, but that was always out of bravado, or when she was wounded. For a woman to witness events such as these and show nothing, this was unprecedented.

My confusion was compounded by a moment which occurred once all trousers were safely buttoned. It concerned the moon-headed fool who called himself the Sultation Kid. The small man, Daniels, quickly returned to his dinner.

But the Kid stood on beside the fire, gazing upwards. Stars glimmered; the moon itself sailed serenely towards the horizon. Finally he seemed to reach a decision, indicated by a flexing of his large shoulders. He gazed down at me and said, with all the pressure of his single yellow eye, 'Son, I reckon I was in error in throwing your weapon. I shall retrieve it.' A noble thought—and he bent to collect his hat. At which point his bare head came down into the light of the fire. There was, everyone could now see, something there, something black—a tattoo. Words were tattooed onto the crown of his head. Around the fire everyone burst once again into crazed laughter. Everyone, that is, except the Mexicans, who were blinded by their sombreros, and myself, unable to read.

And yet I did not want to ask; I did not want in any way to call attention to myself. The Kid, carrying his dripping hat by the brim, rose and stepped out of the circle round the fire. He was beyond being further offended. In the darkness he could be heard cursing, but softly, as though we should only guess at his great difficulties.

As I lay in my bedding, which was augmented by blankets the cook Chowder had supplied, I wondered what these tattooed words might have been. My thoughts tilted and ran, and soon I was wondering also what the words Stronson's finger had written in the dust said. It seemed as I lay there beneath the curved hand of the heavens, with starlight pricking me, and the moon falling, that I had wandered into a circle of knowledge, where everyone knew the meanings except me. As I pondered on this I saw that rather than a circle it was a trail. The cook called Chowder knew my Daddy, knew me; knew our lands. He worked for Stronson, maybe even knew Stronson. It was painful to me, this knowledge of Stronson and my Daddy being in the same narrow place, squeezed up together there inside the tall head of the cook. This picture made my anger come surging through me and I had to turn my thoughts from it.

The stars pricked me. All about I could see the shapes of the sleeping men, each of them snoring according to a distinctive pattern. Beyond, the smell of the cattle came, something large and firm, proof that good existed in the world, that peace might one day be found.

My thoughts eddied.

I saw Henry Stroud kneeling in his own blood, raising his head to speak desperate to me. I saw the coward Stronson standing by my fire with his rifle. I saw the rock with Moses' face on it, staring out, timeless, over the lands.

I saw Spoons, looking in over the roof of the burger bar to find me.

High above, a dark shape passed against the bright pattern of the stars.

She never liked burgers or fried potatoes or anything that Henry Stroud might have cooked her. Food in truth was made too much of—'You can eat the air,' she said, 'if you have to.' She always tried to eat pure, and was constant in an aversion to chocolate, which, to be honest, hardly ever came our way. Nevertheless the skin of her cheeks and forehead continued to pustulate like the roughest of broken country, and red flowers bloomed there. She hated all mirrors. But she was so lovely to look upon.

Yes, hers were the loveliest eyes to gaze into, she was the most lovely thing to hold on the earth entire. And to be held by. As rain made shining bubbles upon windows, as cars growled upon the endless highway, I would lie in Spoons' arms and she would sing us up to high heaven.

She must have seen me, one night, when Henry Stroud

had clicked the padlock on the gate; from across the road called Jervois, must have watched me climb to my rooftop bed. I did hear some noises—then a face appeared above the wooden rim. A woman, and climbing directly into the only place that was mine in the world. If she had been a man I would have pushed her back, stomped her fingers. But a woman. She sat straight down as though she had a right and nodded appreciatively as she looked about her. Then her eyes went up to the spread of the stars. Her back was against the low wooden rim and she drew her knees up and hugged them.

When her gaze came down, like a falling moon, I could not meet it. And so she established her ongoingness in that place. I had never been enclosed with a woman before and was all confusion—if I had had a flower I would have presented it to her; or begun to ask a thousand questions. Instead I grew smaller and attempted to disappear. When she had sat for an hour, a chill wind passed and she spoke. She said, 'Share me a blanket.'

If she had been a man.

In the morning when I climbed down, she stayed. I had heard her during the night relieving herself into the plastic container, which was a terrible sound, and when I climbed down I was horrified that her water was mixed in there with mine. I did consider leaving the container, but I knew this would be observed by Mr Stroud and so I toted it and continued as usual. No further word had passed between us since her demand. We made no agreement. She rested in her corner. But there was a glance, as I went over the rim, and I understood that she would make no sound and would not be discovered; that she had those skills which make discovery a matter of choice.

Seated on Henry Stroud's high chair I thought of her,

lying there in the night above me. The music came through swoony from the comfortable room and I wondered if she heard it. This was an alarming thought. Henry Stroud never claimed the music as anything he owned and I had gone freely inside it, made it a room that I was in, and that was my self's room, which was known only by me, with my own feelings spread open into its every corner. And above me now she was lying.

When at the end of the night's work I climbed back into the precinct of the roof, I was cautious. Henry Stroud had driven away quite readily and I was sure he was not aware that anything in my rooftop world had changed. And it seemed that this was so. She was still there, in her corner. Was this how she had passed the whole day? As soon as the sound of Henry's car receded, she rose and utilised the water can. She saw me cowering from this and laughed. Her relief took an extended period to complete and during this time she held my eyes. From that moment forth she knew everything about me and could make me do her will. I was not unhappy about this.

She came on her knees towards me. She had not adjusted her clothing and she held my eyes. Then she forced my gaze down. So I looked. 'I'm your Eve,' she said. It was many years before I understood this remark as my Daddy had never given me a knowledge of the Holy Bible. In fact her name was Judy Spooner, though that too I did not know for some time. 'Let's have your hand.'

She took me by the wrist and guided me.

And so I became her boy, to help her, and follow her, and be taught by her about the way those who were not born to it might nevertheless live in that world that has burgers but no cattle. It was Spoons who first made me talk. I had listened for so many years, and tried to learn and do the right thing, but Spoons made me give her something from inside myself. Once you have been asked for what is in you, there is no going back.

But none of that happened immediately.

What happened immediately was that my hand brought to me the knowledge that there was a hidden interior to the world. I recoiled upon learning this but Spoons' grip was firm, she had me by the eyes and so I was forced to learn. 'I'm your Venus,' she said. This statement pleased her and she repeated it, and then sang it, over and over; she sang it as a song, the first of many. Then she said, 'Okay, that'll do. I've gotta get something to drink. Come on, let's get going.'

I had become deeply attached to the confines of the burger bar and to be unlocking the padlock filled me with alarm. Now I was out in the city and could feel it alive all around me. I wanted to go slowly and see, to tiptoe through the dark, but Spoons was thirsty. I heard the road called Jervois fall behind us, but there was another road, and then another. Dwellings exactly like Mr Stroud's stood shoulder to shoulder, repeating themselves in every direction and I knew I would soon be lost, and stopped. Spoons returned to me. 'I'll take you back,' she said, and when we ran on she had my hand.

Holding my stinky fingers.

The noises of the city, which was sleeping, were, now that I was out among them, reasons to jump within my skin and be watchful. A slamming door, a roaring car, sirens which passed from one point of the compass to the next. Dogs barking. A distant dog would bark and then one nearby would answer. What were they saying, that we were coming? Was one of those dogs Blackie? How far away was he? Overhead, the barks went back and forth and we ran below. Sometimes Spoons would stop and we would be silent, and crouch behind parked vehicles.

Then she said, 'Shhh.' I followed her up a path beside one dwelling—I understood that we had passed from the commonly used part of the city to a place that one person had ownership of, though there had not been any advice of this. She whispered, 'There's no dog here.' We crouched—above our heads the windows were dark. Near the ground, her hand went into an opening between the boards which ran there and she produced a plastic bottle, which she held as we crept to the rear of the house. There, from a tap, she ran water, and drank. I drank also. The water tasted. But I realised I had been deeply thirsty. Then she returned the bottle, empty, to its place, and we returned to the common roadway, and walked away, now slowed by our bellies. This had been a routine activity for her, I saw this, it was an everyday thing that she did.

But for me it was like the most thrilling adventure. Walking at her shoulder, with the night city a live thing that had you inside it. The dwellings were even spaced on either side and made a kind of canyon. In each one, people were sleeping; upon every hand. There were people everywhere here, all of them strangers. They might at any moment emerge and have to do with us—shoot off their guns. Except that I knew that there were no guns in the city. I had anyway been all my life a handler of guns. I was not afraid of guns. It was the people. I was afraid they would all rise up from their bedding and that I would have to see them. That was it: that I would have to see people, a big herd of them like cattle staring at me to see what I would do.

Spoons led me by the hand and I let her. The streets went between the dwellings like a river, bending here and there but always going on. 'There,' she said and I saw that she had brought me back to the burger bar. How spectral it looked in the night, glowing white, with the coloured pipes of neon flashing so that every time you looked away you had to look back. It filled me with feeling and I was content to gaze upon it but Spoons tugged at my hand and said, 'Where d'you want to go?'

I could feel an impatience in her. I wanted to stay right there, with the burger bar in clear sight. But I said, 'To the ocean.'

'Yeah, okay,' she said, and led me away.

Downhill we went, slowly at first and then running, this time the street was straighter and so I was able to keep the image of the burger bar, glowing, in the back of my head, and not worry that I would find it again.

In the middle of the roadway stood a metal barrier. Cars were stopped all about, but no people. I could sense them in their houses. But here they did not press so tightly as, before us, there was a long strip of water.

I could smell the ocean, and hear it. Not as vividly as at the beach where Mr Stroud had found me, but enough. We walked on concrete and then went down concrete steps, and sat in a little bay just above the dark line which showed where the water had splashed to.

Spoons sat beside me holding her knees. The hard cold of the concrete. The water heaving and slopping. And room. How I craved room, since I had been in the city; how I craved a distance to look out into. This was not the ocean free, here there were concrete walls about it and, in the distance, more houses—I could see their lights. But the eye could run out.

Waves came in and splashed and fell back. To one side a boat was tethered and on the water it went up and down like the head of a horse. It ran out to the end of its tether and then was jerked back. From behind us came the hissing of a street light. Moths flew to it. A large moth landed by Spoons' foot and we both looked down on its eyes, which were glowing red like charcoals from a fire.

She put her head on my shoulder.

It was such a marvellous weight, and the ache it gave me was such a pleasurable ache. The water splashed a little higher and we were forced to shift up one step. I waited. She was looking at the distant houses. Her neck was stiff and she worked it. I waited. Then she put her head back on my shoulder and I felt my heart lie down as though it had finally found its bedding.

Into my shoulder she said, 'So tell me where you came from.'

Chapter Eight

In the early light I was woken by the sound of rushing water and twisted in my bedding to see the Kid addressing a cactus. His black hat was back on his head and I studied it and saw the hole where the ricochet bullet from my gun had entered. There were fringes on the Kid's jacket and his guns had pearl handles. Everything about him announced him for a fool and I closed my eyes so that he would not call out to me.

Soon there were other noises. I folded my bedding and went to look at the horses.

It was a fine thing after six years to stand next to a horse, with that head that was sometimes above you, two ears cut against the sky, and sometimes down sniffing at your boots. The smell of the horses was something I wanted to stand within. I found an old bay that liked a hard forefinger rubbed between the eyes while a hand stroked up and down the side of her neck; that liked being talked to. When I put my head against her she didn't resist but came back with gentle pressure. This is where Mr Lennox found me and he saw everything with one glance of his trailboss's eyes. He looked for a moment, then said, 'You'll be totin' water for Chowder today.' And walked away.

No horse to ride—I was angry as I looked at his back. But that was good; it reminded me. I told myself, there will be plenty of time for horses. And I set off in search of my gun which, despite the muttered curses of the Kid, had not the night before been found. On my knees I went among the broken pieces of rock, the drifts of fine red dirt that lay about at every hand. The feed was scarce here, the cattle would be foraging widely. But this would not pose a problem: there were no fences.

How sweet it was to be out on the lands again.

The gun was lodged between two rocks and when I slid it into the empty holster on my left thigh a sense of balance returned to me and, walking to the chuckwagon, I heard a song start up in my head, which spoke of Abilene, the prettiest town that he'd ever seen, and though there had never been a town that was pretty to me I nevertheless walked in time with the words and let the pictures they made float in my mind like a cloud. It was a grey day, smelling of rain, and as I came up to the wagon I saw that the hands had all stowed their bedding beneath it, so I took this for an example. The long-faced cook appeared and cast his cold eye on me. I explained how Mr Lennox had assigned me to his use. I was on my knees at the time. He stood over me and said, 'The use of the useless is a mystery not even a genius like the Kid can shine a light on.'

'He said for me to tote water.'

The cook adjusted his long limbs as though pulled by strings from above. 'The water is toted an' he knows it. He's just tryin' to rile me up with your broken arse presence. But we will not be downhearted. Come on out of there, Mr Dog, an' let us see what might be done with you.' I stood and faced him. He really was so skinny you thought he might snap. But the force of a man is not in his body. His hair stood out from his head like tall grass; I saw that he had brushed it upwards, and this was a strangeness, that someone who already stood at an altitude to his fellows might seek greater height. 'Maybe you could shoot more turkey?' He considered this and I saw him reject it. The meat of his head was so thin you could detect every movement beneath its surface. Now a fresh notion came to him: he put a thoughtful finger to his temple. 'Did you ever set your eyes on a Victrola, Dog-boy?'

'My Daddy had one.'

'Your Daddy—why so he did. So he did.' The cook nodded as though in recognition, but his eyes were full of a strange kind of gloating and I saw now that this had been his purpose, to bring my Daddy into the conversation. 'So you are familiar. Very good. Yes, I think that will be the correct way to employ you. Now wait here an instant.'

He climbed the wooden steps and entered the body of the wagon, which swayed as he moved inside. I attempted to put myself at ease, gazing about as though the passing clouds were of interest to me and sang silently the song about Abilene where the women there don't treat you mean. But that is a sad song, it is a song about happiness which exists, but at a remove, at a distance, over the hills and far away, and I was dogged as I heard its words by a weariness about the many miles I would have to trudge before I again felt the urge to name a thing as pretty. In truth, my years in the city had opened a hunger in my heart for the soft warmth of love. I had been treated mean, but now I was gone from that life and all I could see about me were miles of dirt.

The cook emerged carrying a box of polished wood above which there stood a black horn—a Victrola in prime condition. Tenderly he placed this arrangement on the top step of his wagon. Then he poured water for me to wash my hands, supervised their drying, then returned to the wagon's interior to retrieve the musical disks. There were seven of these, which was five more than my Daddy had owned and I stared at them as though they might be treasure. 'Now, Mr Dog, your duty is to make sure that no destroying sunlight should fall on these disks, because that makes them into soup plates, and that they do not fall, 'cause they will then shatter—as you well know.' I nodded. 'But I want that you are reminded because then when I kill you down you won't dyin' say to me you was not advised.' Again I nodded. I was familiar with the loss which accompanied the breakage of one of these disks, as my Daddy had once possessed a third example and on starry nights he would try to tell me, without success, what he had heard but would now never hear again. If ever a stranger happened to come into our realm my Daddy never failed to enquire if he knew the whereabouts of any disks that might be had, but the answers were like so many puffs of wind, which only ruffle your hair.

'Before you lower the needle,' the cook said to me, 'you shout out the name of the music we are going to share. Now, don't you overwind that. It's seven turns and no more, on pain of death. Shut one eye when you're lowerin' the needle and if you think you're going to sneeze, wait an' get it over with. Okay, now.'

He had a potato in his hand and a knife for peeling, held steady and waiting for the music to commence. I had the tone arm pinched tight between two fingers and was about to initiate the descent of the sharp needle when he said, 'Wait!'

I stood back. The disk was spinning and I knew that if I did not place the needle soon the seven-times-wound spring would uncoil before the final groove was reached, thus making the music wind down, sounding like your own death experienced prematurely. But I wanted no distraction during the lowering. 'You did not announce the name of the music,' said the cook and nodded towards the centre of the disk where there was handsome lettering.

'I cannot read that,' I said. And now I saw that this again had been something the cook had anticipated. Truly, he had thoughts in that skinny head of his.

'Ah,' he said, nodding. 'I see. So bring that here. Yes, each time, bring the disk to me and tilt it to my eye. Yes, like, that. Alright, *The Dancin' Devil Blues as presented by Memphis Mama Deacon*. Alright, you may commence. No, don't stand on that side, come around here, so I can see you're gonna place that needle right. No, no, closer—oh, not so close! Slowly, now! Wait! No, the spring is half-unwound, wait until the turntable comes to rest, then wind again. Is those disks in the shade?'

So we proceeded, with the cook all the while holding the first potato and the sun always rising in the sky. Out on the lands, the cattle had now spread and all I could see was the swelling cloud of pale dust which rose from them, and the horsemen, upright, moving slowly about like attendant spirits. How I wished I was there. But then that shining needle at last was allowed by the cook to fall into the first of the deep-cut grooves.

From within the horn came a voice the like of which I had never heard. If the oldest tree which grows in the driest, meanest corner of this sorry ball of dirt was to utter a parched moan before finally sheddin' its last leaves it would not sound more heartsick, more will-broken, more lost and gone forever than Memphis Mama Deacon in her hour of revelation.

Oh I hates to have my feet
Settle on the floor
How I hates to have my feet
Settle on the floor
My shoes is just coffins
Cause ma baby don't dance me
No more.

Was she old, Memphis Mama Deacon? Was she pretty? Where was she now in this world, that I could ride to her, kiss her poor feet and soap them with the softest hands. There with clouds gathering in the skies and the cook calmly peeling potatoes, I broke down, the rains fell within me and, seated upon the worn wooden step of the chuckwagon I held my head and cried.

I cried for my Daddy, and my Mama, and for Memphis Mama and for the man she had so carelessly lost. I wept for Henry Stroud who I left dying, and the dog Blackie, and for the loss of the swoony music which had come to me from the comfortable room. I wept for Judy Spoons who had sent me from her lovin' arms.

All of which I saw had occurred to the cook's great satisfaction. When my eyes cleared I saw that he was calmly knifing away the skin of his next potato, watching me all the while. To cry beneath the eye of a watching face is a test. Will you still your tears? Or will you cry on, because your grief is real and nothing matters? Or will the watcher cry too? The cook was too skinny, a tear would have squeezed the last drop from him and so he stood and allowed me my time, which was a quantity he measured with an eyedropper. Then he spoke.

'Your Daddy was shot down,' he said, 'an' your Mama already many years gone and never heard of. And you took yourself off from these lands like a coyote that got its tail in the fire. Be so good as to place that needle again, would you.'

So Mama Deacon spoke again, and the result was the same.

Oh he whirl me up and he show me
That golden fire

111

Yes he whirl me up, make me
Feel that golden fire
Without he dance me
I be drawn out
Like a wire.

And the result was the same; and yet it was more so. The tears were no release to me. Instead they burned and my cheeks began to swell. I could feel them being coloured red and this brought to my mind the cheeks of Spoons who was all flamed up by a wrong attitude to the world—that was what she told me—and on the wooden steps I felt I had joined her in this perspective, that the world was too wrong for me or I too wrong for it and that I would always be outside the world and that now I would be outside and alone.

Chowder the cook peeled steadily and the potatoes made a hollow plop like a frog as they dropped into his bucket. After I had finally reduced myself to sniffling he said, 'An' you came walkin' up out of these lands with three turkey to hide behin' an' hardly sayin' a word an' lookin' at everything as though it's a poison to you—be so kind as to place that needle once more.'

'Sir,' I said, 'you are a cruel kind of man.'

'It speaks!' said the cook. 'Lookee, lookee. But, yes, son, you are right, I am a cruel kind of man an' not many will admit to it, though in their hearts they all of them are. It's a mean ol' world an' don't you forget it. Now lower that needle and feel it go deep into you where the last drop of happiness is waiting to fall, there's a good boy.'

My finger was shaking but I did as I was bid and so Memphis Mama Deacon said again what she had to say.

Now my children stare me
To a puddle
On the floor
Yeah, my children stare me down
To a puddle
On the floor
You can send in the Devil
Cause ma baby don't
Dance me no more.

Perhaps it was because he had named it so but inside me the thing that he described seemed to be happening, the last golden drop of happiness in me hung like a bubble on a windowpane and gathered and then, pricked by the shining steel of that needle, began to slide. And the wails which came out of me were never to be stopped, as I wailed I heard the sound and knew that for miles around every living thing knew of my torture and was broken down by it.

'All done?' said the cook. 'Every last drop? I think we can believe so. Now listen to me, Mr Dog: with all of that gone, when you look inside, what is that you see?'

'Nothin'.'

'I don't believe so.'

So, operating as his creature, that could do no more than as instructed, I looked inside. There seemed only to be whiteness in there, a pale fog that was itself evaporating. Things that were finally disappearing.

Now the cook said, 'Chester Farlowe, son: don't you see just a tiny fist?'

Oh, I knew what he meant! Instantly, yes, there was in me a fist, clenched tight there in my chest, except that it was not in any way tiny. It was blood red, dripping, and as I studied

113

it swelled. My teeth bit upon each other and sweat popped from my brow.

'He shot down your Daddy,' said the cook.

He said this so low that for a second I was not sure I had rightly heard. When I looked at his face the little mouth was squeezed tight as though to prevent anything coming out. How this cook did control what went in to him and what went out. Let others eat potatoes and be thickly layered about. The cook was, as Mama Deacon said, drawn out like a wire and everything made him quiver. Now he said the words again, this time I was watching his thin lips and I saw the words come, each one a little parcel which unfolded and had other words inside it. 'He crept up behind a cactus and shot your sweet Daddy down.'

To say this with me in my condition was adding fuel to a roaring fire and he knew it. 'He didn't call his name. He didn't speak a word. Like a dirty dog, Mr Dog, he worked his way downwind so that not even a tiny sound would come and he pumped a round into the breech. He was on his tippy-toes like a filthy night creeper and put the sights of his gun in the middle of your Daddy's back. With you standin' by. A boy standin' there with his mouth hanging open and having to see. D'you remember that, Mr Dog?'

I stared into the cold eyes of the cook and, whatever had happened in the past, my mouth was open now. Had he been there? How did he know? My head was spinning like a flicked coin—and even as it went round I knew there was something wrong with his account. But I had no chance to dwell upon this, as he was speaking again. He held my eyes and he said, 'The coward Stronson snuck up on your Daddy and killed him down so that he fell into your arms. And you held the weight of him, dyin'.'

I remembered again that dark bird speeding away from me over the lands and all I could see was red.

'He is a coward,' said the cook. 'A back-shooter, Chester. He took your Daddy away from you with all the love you ever had.' Oh, how my head was spinning! 'He deserves to die. Kill him, Chester. Rip his heart out and squeeze it till it runs.'

Chapter Nine

The report on me that Chowder the cook gave to trailboss
Lennox must have been a good one, for, after evening chow
on the third day, I was told that in the morning I would be
given a horse and that I might ride the herd. And so I found
myself once more up on the spine of an animal, which rocked
me slowly as we walked at the rear of the spread of browsing
cattle. At the rear is where the dust hangs and is always the
province of the greenhorn, but I simply pulled my bandana
up over my nose and made the best of it. To be carried by
four legs in the company of cattle, this is a kind of heaven.

The horse was an old bay name of Bess. I never touched
her once with my spurs; I let her have her head. I felt, after the
pain the cook Chowder had raised in me, that every simple
moment must be dwelled within and I rode herd like it was
all the destiny I had ever hoped for.

On the lands around, the cactus stood and also the
mountain, with glimpses of snow about its cloud-bothered
peak.

The sun's hand on everything.

We settled the cattle down in the last of the light and took
our horses one by one to the tying place and straggled back
to the fire, where the stew smell came pungent. As chance
would have it I straggled beside Miss Peet and her womanly
presence in that place was such a marvel to me that I found
words and for once spoke uncalled for.

'Was you born to these lands, Miss?' I politely inquired.

She tilted her head a little as we walked, inclining an eye towards me. 'Don't you be seein' anythin' that ain't actually there, son.' She was somewhat bow-legged, as most cowboys are, and walked with a saddle-sore roll. 'Don't let your head run away. We is out here on the lands and is lucky to be so. Just take a lick o' the salt when it's there in front of you.'

'Thank you, m'am.'

'My pleasure,' she said.

Just to hear a woman's voice, this made me glad to be in my boots. I wanted then to capture a tiny inhalation of her and it may have been that my nostrils whistled a little, for she glanced at me again. 'Everythin' you take in, then that is in you and is what you is, boy. Be careful what you is, because then you has to live with it.'

Then we came to the fire and she went east and I went west and soon were raising the spoons of stew with the best of them. But in my mind we both of us continued round the fire and came together and, side by side, walked on again. Which was a prospect which made my poor heart ache.

That night in my bedding I lay under the blanket of stars and longed for the touch of a hand. To be in another's arms. But I had had the horse under me, had been rocked through endless hours, and so I fell into a dreamless sleep and woke only when the dawn birds were all shouting out their names.

And in this way a number of days rolled by.

On the eighth day I was sent by boss Lennox to shoot turkeys and I rode away from the herd and into a long canyon where the echoes were like pistol shots. I loaded my guns.

Exercising care, I expended only three bullets upon the three birds I needed, and these were laid upon a rock in the shade. Then I tethered Bess and, taking myself off somewhat distant, stood maybe twenty paces from a tall cactus which had arms to the side like any man. My fingers tingled. 'Draw!' I shouted, and went for my guns. As the echoes ran back and forth from the canyon walls, one of the arms shivered and then fell. But an arm-shot was no use to me and I fired and fired until there was a ragged hole in the central trunk where I thought a man's heart might be.

What a strange game this was! Your mouth said 'Draw' but your fingers were twitching. What went faster through your head, the message to the mouth or the message to the fingers? If the fingers moved first, you had cheated and were a coward who could claim no glory. But if the mouth moved first, why then it seemed that he, in front of you, would have an advantage, as you had to do the two things and he only the one, and he would likely cut you down. How would you feel as you saw the bullet shot from the hole of the barrel and coming towards your eye and knowing that behind it everything was black? I was musing upon these things when there was a sound behind me and I spun, hands at the ready.

There framed by the rim of the canyon stood the Sultation Kid. 'Easy, son,' he called, 'just lift your hands away and no harm will come to ya.' We faced each other, tense, fingers frozen in the air. My thighs with the holsters tied to them were taut. Flies buzzed. A trickle of sweat ran down slow from under my hat. In front of me the shape of the Kid was like a trigger, urging me to draw. 'Easy,' called the Kid again and I controlled myself, and my hands lifted, trusting that his would do the same.

Now the Kid ambled towards me. 'Thought for moment I was gonna hafta cut ya down there, son,' he said. 'Whoa. It's a month at least since I done face down a man—then

118

doncha feel like you just gotta ease yaself.' Directly before me he unbuttoned and commenced to darken the dust. I was receiving splashes and, as politely as I could, went to investigate the state of my turkeys. They continued to be dead. The echoes of the splashing were kind of maddening. The dead eyes made tiny holes that you couldn't look into, buzzed by flies. Now a heavy hand fell on my shoulder. 'Listen son I gotta tell ya,' the Kid said, 'I seen what ya done an' it ain't pretty.' His one-eyed gaze went along the canyon floor till it found the foot of my cactus, up which it ran. He inclined his eye at the arm-shot and shook his head. 'By the time ya got around to pluggin' one in his vitals,' he said, 'the angels'd be strappin' wings onta ya.' Up close, there was a rank odour which accompanied the Kid, the congealed sweat of a thousand quick-draw face downs. 'Ya gotta do it like this.' Without apparent movement his gun appeared in his hand and loosed a bullet—a sturdy cactus showed a hole clean through. His hand was still on my shoulder. In quick succession he shot out three of the flies that circled the biggest turkey. A low-flying bird exploded in the air then landed thud between my boots. Together we looked down. 'Then everythin's dead,' he said, letting out a sigh, 'an' when ya ride off into the sunset ya trail all them deads behind ya. The deads worship ya, do ya know that, boy? You was the one, fur them, their destiny, an' they come trailin' along behin' an' no matter how far ya ride out into the heat o' the desert they come along behin', sayin' ya name and askin' ya for water.' He leaned his weight on me now and put his heavy head on my shoulder.

I too bowed my head; I closed my eyes. The Kid's touch was, like the touch of every hand that ever came to me, a thing that roused my heart. So we stood there together, the killer and the boy destined to kill, in the echoing canyon, under the bouncing echo of the gunshots, the dead turkeys lying, the bird crumpled between my boots, the flies buzzing.

Over the succeeding days the Sultation Kid took time to instruct me in the expert use of the weapons I had inherited from my father. We shot up every cactus for miles. He improved not only my aim but also the speed of my draw. 'It's the little things,' he told me, and had me position my open hand just so. He rubbed turkey fat into the linings of my holsters—this I discovered was part of the polecat pong which sang around him—so they were slick to the touch. He explained me how to set up your high noon at sundown, so that you could get the sun behind you. Well, I knew that one.

He also was kind enough to talk me in detail through his many killings but these need not be further recounted.

The herd was so large that at times it seemed as though the whole land was moving around you. A sea of backs with long, shapely horns. Calves calling. The smell of a herd is herbaceous and warm and behind it you ride inside a cloud that is so thickly complete that no other life seems to exist.

Bess was a fine horse and, mounted upon her, within the shade of my hat I would have been happy to stay. The heels of the cattle, the flick of hoof. A beast snorting at a snake. The herd parting to round a tall rock, then flowing together again. It was a slow world where anything you were able to wish up could be the place you were in—in my head I saw the man who went down, down, down, I saw the burning ring of fire. I saw the blue bayou. I laid out the deck of cards, from a jack to a king.

I could have stayed there.

Sometimes a bird would catch my eye as, from the horizon, it came speeding low. The upper air was full of clouds, their shapes made stories too, and the wind brought pictures also. The herd jostling as it rumbled slowly. Bess's steady walk. Those low birds came and passed over and went away rearward, dark into the lands. In my mind's eye those birds flew on, never resting, pulling all thoughts behind them.

The Kid could shoot but anyone could see he was no rider. The Mexicans were the riders. Beneath their great hats they nodded as though in sleep. But their portion of the herd was never ragged, it flowed like one thing, that there was no need to shape.

In the distance I could often make out the upright form of Miss Peet. The trailboss favoured her and so she rode ahead of the dust. Though at the evening washtub her face was streaked as any.

She was pleasant to walk beside.

One night after chow she spoke into the fire. Loud: 'Mr Lennox, I'm gonna check the off-side shoe on Stubbins, that pony is I reckon gettin' set to shed an iron.'

'I didn't see it,' said the trailboss, maybe a little insulted. But he was a close-controlled man. 'Mr Dog, you accompany Miss Peet and hold the heada that hoss, would you be so kind.'

Now the Kid spoke. 'It's powerful dark out there, Miss Peet, I think I had best come instead, case of Injuns.'

'You hold your water,' said Miss Peet curtly. This remark produced a round of guffaws. The Kid eyed me across the flames. But he stayed where he was and Chowder the cook stepped in to heap more stew upon his plate, which settled the matter.

So to my pleasure I found myself walking out beneath the stars with the cowgirl.

The matter of the loose horseshoe was quickly settled; 'I must tell Mr Lennox that he was correct,' remarked Miss Peet. 'Well, it's cool out here away from that jumpin' fire. Think I'll find me a rock to set upon.' Which she did. I myself was in no haste to get back to the fire, anyways I had been assigned to stay with her. So I sat also, which seemed to be acceptable. Immediately a song started up in my head, that one I had heard so frequent of late, which had the fiery ring, where the flames get higher. Sat there beside her in the silence with that song singing loud, and the night sky above us seeming to be full of light that drew the eye. The standing outlines of cactus. The mountain's broken head. Miss Peet too was looking upwards and then I saw her finger rise and indicate a great dark shape which, flashing, moved high against the bright pattern of the stars. She spoke low. 'What do you think, Mr Dog,' she said.

Her finger moved so as to hold upon the shape and after a time of consideration I said, 'My Daddy always told me they were angels.'

'Did he,' said Miss Peet. 'Angels.' And she continued to study the shape as though the idea was something that might be toyed with. Or was that me, that would be played with like a toy? We were not set close beside one another but, out in such a vast dark, to be within a shout is as close as sticks in a fire. I wished then to see her face.

But her face was something Miss Peet kept to herself, beneath a low hat and behind a bandana. Especially her eyes were never to be found.

'Your Daddy,' she said.

I took now her voice and tried to grasp what could be known from it. It was clear even to a slow-moving animal like myself that the horse Stubbins had never had any loose shoe. Miss Peet had wanted to be here with me and as I fully grasped this truth my boy's heart loudly announced its presence there inside my chest. 'That's what my Daddy said,' I said. Which was the kind of empty response that would, I knew, have earned me a wet tongue in the ear from Judy Spoons, who demanded that if a game was to be played it be played full out. 'Is you from these parts, Miss Peet?'

'What else did your Daddy tell you?' she asked. 'For example, about the railway lines.'

'The railway lines goes to the city,' I said.

This remark, which was no more than the truth, nevertheless hung in the night air and after a moment I found I was sitting upright with my spine erect and a low tingle ringing there like a little bell. Miss Peet did not speak. Her hand, which had been withdrawn to her lap, now came forth again and this time it was extended towards me. So I took the hand, and we were joined. From the hand I took immense things, great promises like an entire new land. But there was no caress. Her hand was dry and its fingers merely held mine. I felt then how chill the night was and that I was a single object upon a cold stone under the silent stars.

'Angels that fly in the sky and trains that run to the city,' said Miss Peet. 'In the distance great things could be observed, whereas we at the watering hole saw only hole and water.' This sounded as though she was repeating the words of a sage or perhaps the Bible. My Daddy did that sometimes. The sense that knowledge was a possession of every man I met, that I was the sole and lonely-walking centre of ignorance, this sensation was my constant companion. And yet I had been to the city. I had seen. But I was no more than a rampant parade of impulses, some of them murderous, and I knew it.

Miss Peet once again pointed to a shape among the stars,

this time much further away, and when she was done pointing her hand returned to her lap. I felt its loss keenly, and was at once strongly reminded of every loss I had ever experienced. How happiness can come and go, like the swinging of a door. Nevertheless the connection that her hand had made was not entirely broken. I could feel her body there beside mine and even as a centre of ignorance I knew there was something in her that wanted something of me.

'Do you think, Mr Dog,' she said, 'that if I told you my name you might be persuaded to tell me yours?'

'My name is Chester Farlowe,' I said readily.

'And mine is Leah. Tell me, Chester Farlowe, why it is that you who knows what an angel looks like when it sits upon a runway would return to these lands?'

These words made me shake and I felt as though the rock I was sitting upon would split under me and that the fire inside the mountain would at any moment come pouring down. Everyone here seemed to know me for what I was and I wondered then if I had some mark upon me that all could see. Miss Peet observed the confusion she had caused and once again she extended her hand. But I left it lying on the rock and instead I turned to look her full in the face.

Her face there in the dark was shaded by her hat which she wore low. But now she tilted her head up and allowed me to see. How lovely she was. She had what I believe is called a heart-shaped face, with dark curls all massed about and her nose and lips delicately sculpted, so that you immediately thought that this is what we human creatures were intended to be. I understood that she was what Judy Spoons had enviously referred to as 'a gorgeous creature' and that to be so lovely was a weight in the world; an inescapable burden. I understood that she was risking something by letting me gaze upon her, and that with each moment that passed she was risking more. Down, down, down and the flames going higher—down without end I went. Miss Peet sat before my gaze and let me fall.

Then she smiled and instantly I saw how much older than me she was, five year at least, and how every word that had been spoken on this night and everything I had seen had been known beforehand by her and that now I would be alone within the ring of fire and she would be far away from me on the back of her herd-leading horse.

'Mr Dog,' she said gently.

'Yes, Miss Peet.'

'You shouldn't worry so much.'

These words made my heart soar, though I knew it was unwise. Oh my heart went like an eagle on an updraught, up, up, and the lands spreading below. 'But I would like you to think,' she said. 'Why did you return here?'

I knew the answer to this and it rose at once to my lips. But then some sense of the way the game was played came to me and I held my thick tongue.

Now from the direction of the fire, where my thoughts had never once been in the time we had sat together, there came a volley of shouting and then, suddenly, a shot. Followed by frightened silence. Then boss Lennox said clearly, 'When he wants his hair parted he'll ask for it. Now sit down, Kid.'

Miss Peet didn't have to say that we should be returning, we both knew this and rose together. It is sweet to the heart when such unison occurs. She looked across at me, and this time there was no smile, which made my heart go even higher. Up, up, up and down, down, down. She said, 'And tell me please, when we speak again, Mr Dog, where it is you think that the pylons are going.'

Chapter Ten

'The day will come,' my Daddy said, 'when you look at the mountain and think of her. You will see her in the way your horse walks, and you will smell her in the smell of your lariat, and you will look out over the lands and not see anything but her, everywhere you look and nowhere that can be seen.' As I rode at the rear of the herd these words rode shotgun with me. Sometimes I could see Miss Peet far ahead, across the humped backs of the cattlebeasts, shimmery through the cloud of dust which hung over them. She looked in the distance like any cowboy. Then in a hole in the air her face would appear before my eyes, with astonishing clarity, and just as quickly be gone. Songs came into my head, voices also, and places, and the sound of places, and eyes. The sense that Judy Spoons had jealous eyes which saw down upon me was overwhelming. 'You left me because I was a fat slag,' her eyes said, 'and now that you've found yourself a pretty one you're going to forget you ever had this poxy old fat-cunted slag.' It's not true, Spoons, I would protest, I will always love you first. But these words had a hollow ring.

There was a song she liked to hit me with, about a spoonful. When she sang this she sounded old and hard—as old and mean and hard used as she could manage. Her eyes would go slitty and her voice would rough up like a snaggle-toothed saw. I didn't know this then but she was trying to sound as much as possible like Memphis Mama Deacon. Sometimes, lifted by her singing, she would rise to her feet. We would be under an overpass, with cars going by and Spoons with her hand on herself. This what that song's about, she would growl at me, this spoonful right here. Everybody wants the spoonful—that spoon, that spoon, that spoonful.

But sometimes she sang it soft, calculated to make me fall into her eyes, in which I always obliged. But one little spoon of my precious love, save you from the desert sands.

Spoons took me everywhere in Auckland city and always she made sure that we were never caught. She knew how to get food and okay water and how to sneak in to the movies. There was nothing she didn't know and this was a thing that she spoke of, how there was nothing left for her to know. 'That's why I have you, punkin face, so I can do everything all over again.' But sometimes she looked old and wearied.

I tried to question her. 'Oh, question time today,' she would say, and come up with things like, 'I came down the river in a boat of reeds.' Or, 'One day they was diggin' a new road and there I was, a buried toad, with dirt all over me, which I never shook off.'

One morning we caught a bus, which was rare because you had to have actual money, and out the window I saw how the city went on and on and everywhere you looked there was more of it, all going on the same. The picture came to me that the city was trying to cover everything and I wondered if ever I would get back to the lands and would they still be there or covered over? Spoons said, 'What's in your head means they're there.' For once she was serious and I knew then that she cared about the lands and the part of them that still lived inside me.

Now the bus came to where the airplanes were coming down out of the sky and she took me to where we could look through fence wire and see them hit the ground. Smoke burst from the tyres. The wings drooped, tired from the flight. The roar as they stopped being angels and turned into buses was just what you would expect and then they would turn slowly and look at you with their eyes too close together and frankly I was afraid. 'Did you ever be inside one?' I asked her.

'All the way to Dallas,' she said. 'In my ex life. All the way to Port Arthur.'

'Why?'

We were hanging onto the wire of the fence with our fingers, side by side, and the air was full of oil which made a slick down my throat. It was like wanting to sicken to stay there but we stayed and the airplanes came and kept coming and I always wanted to see just one more. She said, 'That was what I wanted. Not to fly, just to be there in America where everything comes from and sing.' Plainly it made her sad to talk about this but I hung on the wire and waited and eventually she spoke again. 'But you have to be pretty before they'll let you sing.'

An airplane roared so that the ground shook but I knew she was hurting and I held her and she let me.

Spoons had holes in her cheeks like one of those little white balls they use for golf and a nose that hung on her face as though it had melted and would soon fall. I see that now. But she made a tent of her hair and when she invited you in why then would you see those things, and anyway when you did they were beautiful because of her eyes. Spoons kept you in her eyes and only a fool wanted to be anywhere else. She was the most precious object that was alive and breathing the air and my thoughts were always of her and what she might want from me. Her eyes were a horse ride of ten thousand days in every direction and if I could ever go in there I never hesitated.

Then when I saw Miss Peet I learned what Judy Spoons saw in me and why she tried to keep me to herself.

We turned from the wire and, with the angels roaring behind us, walked away from the airport. It was a road with no footpath and vehicles streamed past without a break, as though they were one long thing without an ending. But through the fence there was lush grass and then cattlebeasts. 'Could you just round 'em up,' said Spoons, 'an' mob 'em on over to Denver.' This was her making fun of me, which she liked to do. But the smell of the cowshit was carrying me back to the lands.

We walked steadily and went in among the streets and were enclosed by dwellings. Spoons wasn't saying anything and seemed wary so I kept my mouth shut. We walked and walked, going in deeper. Dogs came to gateways to bark at us and when I saw her face her mouth was shut tight. In the near distance airplanes roared. She took us down a path between the dwellings and there was a low fence made of wire with round metal poles that connected. Here we stopped. Spoons put her backside on the fence so that is what I did. But slowly I realised that behind us was what she was seeing.

It was a backyard, with an old vehicle with no wheels, and a cobwebby arrangement of wire that I knew from Mr Stroud's was where you hung your clothes, except that here the wires were all hanging down. 'Tell me,' I said.

'Tell yourself,' she said and she wandered away.

So I studied what could be seen there—a doghouse but no dog, and machines lying and likely broken. The grass growing long. Broken bottles and glass down in there, and maybe little animals. On the roofline an assembly of birds said they were the masters here. Judy Spoons was waiting at the head of the path. She never waited. I looked and looked and when I looked back at the dwelling I saw that she had been a child here; that she was showing me her home. Here under the sound of the airplanes she had learned how to sing and it was this that she was always singing about, which was not anything you could love unless you had nothing else. She loved me truly to let me see this, I knew that, and there in the little pathway between the dwellings I resolved never to be the cause of any longing in her and to always hold her when the lonesome feelings walked out inside her head.

When she saw me looking at her again she turned and headed away, so that I was forced to leave too or be lost among the houses which went on and on in every direction.

One night there had been no food for three days and even Spoons agreed she was hungry. We wandered, me making various suggestions, but I saw she was working on something so finally I just tagged along. Then I saw the wire cage and Henry Stroud's car, and the padlock, and the white building with the clicking neon sign.

We waited outside, Spoons watching carefully up and down the street. When finally we entered we were the only customers. I hung back somewhat but Spoons stepped right up to the counter. 'Burger time, Mr Stroud,' came the call.

There on my high chair a boy was seated and I hated him with an instant hate so pure that it made the white-painted walls sing as though they were electric. He was avoiding our eyes, as I once had, so I had a good look so that if I saw him in the street I would know. Now I received the music which was coming low from the comfortable room and my eyes filled with loss. My head hung as I listened . . . *I'll keep my hand shut tight so when they find me, they'll find the pearl, for Leah*. To the swelling accompaniment of this small opera Henry Stroud appeared and smiled down at us. I wasn't looking but all at once I knew he was there, and then I couldn't look. He would I knew see my hatred of the boy on my chair, and he would see that I had chosen Judy Spoons over him, and his eyes would tell me that I had left him without so much as a goodbye. All the time that music was swelling and my eyes were full.

There was a long moment and I do not know what passed between Henry Stroud and Spoons who was standing there beside me. I was full of shame and that made the hate more intense. Then Mr Stroud spoke down. He said, 'Is that you, Mr Dog?'

I nodded.

His voice was all about my head like a cloud and I was remembering how he had put his fingers in my hair and how his hands had been all I could watch while the music came without ending from the comfortable room. If I could have gone to him I would have. But the high counter was a range of mountains that had never been crossed.

'I guess it's a cheeseburger then,' he said. And he turned his back and began cooking.

Up on the roof of this building I had slept. On that chair I had sat. Once a place has been yours, it is painful when the world changes. All the steps you have taken, which seemed so mighty, fold to a thing you could put in your pocket and all the days run backwards and make you small again. Then here were the burgers, in their paper bags, two for each of us, and a bag of salty chips, and vanilla shakes. On the counter they lay, speaking so strongly to the hole in my stomach, while the white walls buzzed and the radio sang softly and while that boy sat on there on my chair. Spoons elbowed me. 'Aren't you going to speak?'

I looked up. There was his huge head with the bumps

and the dark curls of springy hair. Full of sorrow for myself I opened my mouth and said, low, 'Burger time, Mr Stroud.'

'And happy days, Mr Dog. Happy days to you. You look after this nice lady, now.'

Spoons took the burgers and led us away.

I had hoped he would reach over the counter and put his fingers in my hair. Up there, through the roof of my head, I could feel where he had not. I could feel where his hand had not touched my shoulder; on my back I could feel the shirt which was not the washed-out shirt with the islands and the swaying trees that he had given me. Spoons took us downhill and found a place on a concrete fence to sit while she ate. All I could understand was that I had once had Henry Stroud and now I had lost him. Spoons ate and ate. On the road called Jervois cars went past and people walked. The neon sign of the I Fry clicked on and off in the night. I stared down into the hole in the air and wanted to go somewhere but I couldn't think of where.

Judy Spoons left one burger sitting on the fence beside me and went off into the night.

When I stand now on the planking of my porch and study the clouds, I see the shimmering faces of these people I used to know. Not on the clouds, not like big faces on a movie screen, no, but bigger, and so strongly there for something that I can never exactly catch. The years which stand between me and those faces fold to a little thing that I could put in my pocket and what comes swelling are the feelings that each face carries. I hear movements inside the cabin, I hear the life I have made and see the lands running away from me and the cattlebeasts moving and the men riding after. If I once pause for just a moment all comes sweeping back towards me and falls, like waves falling on a beach, and I am churned, twisted. I tip the dregs of my coffee and watch them drain, dark, into the red dust. My eyes go around the horizon.

No riders.

Part Three

Chapter Eleven

My Daddy had often pondered with me the mystery of the pylons. It was troubling to my little head that there was something he didn't know, a subject that he was not the master of and so, when it was returned to, my heart would pound just a little. 'They always have been there,' he would say, and with his stick draw long, looping lines in the dust so that I was reminded of the wires which hung so heavy in the upper air. 'But there's just somethin' about them that ain't right,' he would say and his brows would stitch together and there was the feeling that if anything moved he would go for his guns.

Sometimes I would entertain the notion that he was afraid of them—was it the pylons? or the wires?—and this thought also brought pounding to my heart. And so to test myself I would when I was out on my own go riding beneath the wire lines and experience the forces which came to me there. My teeth burned. My hair stood out from me.

Once I climbed down from the saddle to place my hand upon the metal foot of a pylon and this made my poor head be filled with every speck of dust and every gust of wind that has ever been blown. I cannot say what I made of the pictures I saw or even what the pictures were, but all I knew was that the city world was connected to our lands by something that would never be understood by those who merely walked upon them. And was drinking from them.

These thoughts from the days with my Daddy came to my mind very strongly in the time which followed my night under the stars with Miss Peet. As I rode behind the herd now I planned what I might say to her when next I was alone in her company.

At nights she was always at the campfire but the tilt of her hat kept her face in constant shadow. Her voice never spoke for her other than as a cowboy who just happened to be a woman. How could she pretend so? This pretending made feelings rise in me like whirlwinds. Would she never glance at me? But her stew was fascinating to her, her hat was always down, her back was always turned.

From the length of my bedroll I measured the distance to where she lay and felt the night to be the greatest ocean which could never be walked upon.

Then the day came when boss Lennox declared he was plumb tired of prairie stew and would I be so kind as to ride out and shoot something tasty for the boys. So in the company of my guns I headed south and was soon far from any human soul. It was a chill day, with a wind that set the tumbleweeds to bowling. Dust rose and made great shapes in the air.

I loosed a bullet at every cactus, shooting from the saddle. The guns flowed into my hands like water and the bullet was gone before I had fully formed the idea to shoot. I was faster than a rattlesnake. No man could stand before me—I knew that. I was a murderous impulse on horseback and the world should cower. I blasted a hornet that flew a line beside me, which is a demanding shot when you are riding full out, and rode on. The lands fell away from me.

High, an eagle stood between me and the sun and I decided to let him live.

I turned tortoises onto their backs and soon had a collection that would make a roast. In the shade of a bowl cactus they wiggled their legs and snapped at each other.

Now the eagle was leading my eye to the western quarter and so it was that on the horizon I spied a standing tower of metal, and the dark lines which ran from it. When I touched the spurs to Bess she went forward willingly and soon the lands were going beneath her reaching feet as though she was drinking them in. Small birds raced alongside. I held my hat with one hand and crouched low. My ears whistled. Riding herd, the horses never are asked to run and so Bess was baring her teeth, carrying me as though I was no more than a speck of dust. We came up on the wires and were beneath them and through before I knew it.

To the north great open lands lay as though you might ride hard all your life and never reach the limit of them. I watched the shadows of clouds pass slowly and, spreading my arms, stood in the stirrups and threw my head back.

The wires, when I returned to them, swayed high above in the dirty wind. As we came closer I saw that beneath them was a long, raw strip where nothing stirred. Bare dirt, and not even an ant crossing. Something went along Bess's spine which made a shiver pass beneath me and I climbed down and left her trailing her reins.

Beneath the wires I walked and it was nothing.

In the south the mountain stood and around it the lands which were wide and free of fences. But here, following the wires, was a narrow place like a road, like a channel for an invisible river, where my feet stepped on nothing and the air was as dry and as blue as the endless sky between the clouds. I walked and walked and was soon unable to imagine ever leaving this long path. Between my head and the wires my hat was a heavy impediment and so I removed it and walked on. It was so peaceful here, and the dust fell smoothly from my boots. What good company your stride is, which carries you over the lands—and so I walked and walked and might have walked to that cliff where the world ends if, dead ahead, there had not been the base of the great metal tower.

The sight of it cooled me and I stood, glancing about. Slowly, my hand went to the back of my neck—I watched the hand rise through the air before me. I stood, head slightly forward. Now my teeth commenced to sing and across the curve of my skull the hairs stood like blades of grass and began to wave as though a wind was among them.

Swaying, I knew that the eagle was somewhere high above me, a black memory in the sky. I thought of Bess and saw only her white bones, standing, a skeleton with a shiver. I saw Miss Peet and all her clothes were burned away.

Yes, there within the ambit of the pylon I clearly saw Miss Peet clad only in her natural glory and to her glory I began to sing. There was only one song which would do, and I knew every word of it. Swaying, swaying, blinking my eyes and every loaded word coming to me like a revelation, I released that song which had been held by the world to be drawn upon at this moment.

I gotta go down, go diving in the bay—oooh-hoo
Gotta get a lot of oysters
Find some pearls today—oooh-hoo
To make a pretty necklace for Leah
Lee-ee-ah.

I knew as I sang that the pylon was milking the song from me, I could feel that, and yet I sang all out and would not willingly have stopped. Across the lands my boy's voice was carried by the wires. The mountain heard me. The tiny animals in their holes heard me. Miss Peet riding naked in her warm saddle heard me, heard me singing her name and was

140

moved to turn to the northern quarter and, alone at the head
of the herd, lift her hand and tilt her face up to the sun.

I gotta go deep and find the ones just right—oooh-hoo
I'll bet my Leah will be surprised tonight—oooh-hoo
I'll place the pearls around the only girl for me
Lee-ee-ah.

And in the cities. Up the great blacktop strip and into the
cars which rolled restless on the highways. In the endless
dwellings which had all radios tuned to the pylon station—
in the comfortable room, where Henry Stroud had his feet
warm upon the belly of Blackie the dog, and out on the high
chair which held the boy who had no right; down in the little
bay where the rowboat rocked—everywhere they stopped
and listened. The fishes in the deeps. Spoons in the arms of a
jealousy so keen. The wires snaked inside me and took that
song which is the juice that feeds the world. Stirred by my
feet, the dust danced. There was a crackling. I went for my
guns and, as I sang, I loosed bullets about into the air until
the chambers all were empty.

But something's wrong
I cannot move around—bang
My leg is caught
It's pulling me down—bang
But I'll keep my hands shut tight for if they find me
They'll find the pearl for Leah—bang bang bang.

And now it's over
I'm awake at last
Oh, heartaches and memories from the past
It was just another dream about my lost love

About Leah
Hey, Lee-ee-ah, Leah
Hey, Lee-ee-ah, Leah
Here I go
Back to sleep and in my dreams
I'll be with Leah.

Then, with the emptied weapons still hot in my hands, I lay down at the foot of the pylon and fell into a swoon.

White bones walked about me, offering their broken hearts before them. Silver bullets sped away. Black roses fell through golden air to bounce on the red dirt, and crumble. In the distance a lonesome whistle sounded its long, passing note and as a nation the bones turned and chorused that song.

In the city the cars rolled restless and all the radios played the broken-hearted music which was piping through the bones.

A riderless horse carried its empty saddle out into the badlands.

The air crackled.

Horse teeth, like tombstones, huge green horse teeth, damp horse breath and then the bulging horse eye full of seeing. A wet kiss from thick lips—Bess was nuzzling me and I rose and was led by her away from that place. I could not have said my name. Walking and walking and there was only dust which rose from my boots and then fell again. I was walking bones and had no desire.

I took my emptied guns from their holsters and flung them from me.

Across the lands we walked. I had not the wit to climb up onto her back and so when night fell we walked on. I would have slept in my boots but Bess knew better and so as the stars whirled about overhead I trudged my steady way across the lands and through the dark. We passed the sleeping herd and came to the tethered horses, which is where Bess stopped. Immediately I lay down and was at once gone inside the lonesome whistle song which goes long across the world as the light dies.

Perhaps Bess made a commotion, wanting for water and a nosebag, or maybe it was me lying there which stirred the horses, I cannot say. But the Kid's voice came to me, his teeth in the darkness were as green as Bess's and glowed to my eyes, and his eyepatch pulsed—then his voice came to me, but it was too late and so I saw his open hand come sweeping round to slap me. I heard the hard smack of it and its echo, but felt nothing. 'Dog, Dog, Dog,' he was saying and then I heard him holler: 'This boy has been to the pylons!'

And I sat up and smiled as though I was proud.

They took me to the fire and examined me and poured water over my head. I was smiling around and this made the Mexicans laugh. The scar-faced man, Henley, came across to place a burning coal in my hand and I smiled down at it while smoke rose and the smell of burning flesh filled the air. Lennox threw water over that. Henley said, 'Say I am a girl.'

'You are a girl,' I said, dripping.

'No! Say, I am a silly girl done drink all Daddy's giggle juice.'

I said it to his satisfaction.

They roared with laughter. 'Here, have an apple.' Though it was an onion, I bit deeply and the apple taste was sweet to me. I smiled about and ate my apple down to the core. Henley said, 'This girl will do any man's bidding.'

'Any damn fool's.'

This was Miss Peet and came as a growl from low under

her hat. Oh, Miss Peet! As the thought of her returned to me I blinked and this instantly burned away her clothes.

Well, it was one thing to see her in her glory from miles away but sitting here among the fellows was a vision so shocking to me that I blinked again and now saw only her glowing bones—her skull grinned as her skeleton fingers lifted the spoon of stew to her mouth. Black roses descended slowly through the air about her. My hand went over my eyes and I fell forward, singeing my hair in the fire, which was in part dowsed by Lennox's third application of water.

They carried me to my bedding, tying a rope tight to my ankle so that I should not wander.

I had never thought of Spoons as fat and it would be wrong now to call her so. We did not eat every day and were never still but always walking off such food as we got as this was the only way to get there. But when I saw Miss Peet I understood why this word once came to Spoons.

She had taken me to a place where music was sold, so she told me, though at the time I struggled to understand. We had been before. People were always there, looking, and we were not made welcome. But Spoons tried to stay whenever she could as there was music endlessly playing. She would hold a picture of a particular man and say, 'He knows every heartbreak moment of your lonely life.' He wore a black hat like a dude cowboy and his eyes were shaded from me. This man she was partial to had a name and she would say it as though it gave a secret pleasure: Roy Orbison. 'Roy is the voice of an angel who's found the way home.'

She carried a picture of his face folded in her pocket and would sing to the picture sometimes with me eavesdropping. *Running Scared*, it sounded like our lives.

Spoons liked to keep moving while we were there and I could tell she had something she was turning her back on. She would give me little nudges and we would go to another place in the shop. It was nice to be there with so much music loud in the air but none of the people who all had their heads down seemed to care; they were always looking. I studied up at the places where the music came from, which seemed to be like radios, hung high, but Spoons said no, 'But don't worry about it.' Spoons and I cared and maybe that was why there was always a man who came behind us and said we had to go away. 'Gizza job,' said Spoons.

This was the day that everything happened. 'You look like a real hard worker,' said the man.

'Nah, just real hard,' said Spoons. 'If yas ever had one.'

'Fuckin' likely, lookin' at you.' And his eyes went over her and he laughed.

'Shut your gob, the pus is leaking out,' she said, and dragged me away.

We bent our heads and climbed up the city of Auckland into the wind. It was a chill day and the only place we could think of was Myers Park. We sat close up behind some trees. She had her back against my chest, being held for warmth, and she asked if I thought she was fat. I didn't know what she was talking about.

The words spoken that day all sticking in my memory.

She said, 'Mirror, mirror—tell me.' I could not understand and she said, 'Forget it.'

The sky was grey with cold and the buildings all were closed against us. 'Let's go up the uni,' she said and we set off. Neither of us liked it there, me because I was afraid I would get lost in all the stairways and Spoons because she said she was afraid of running into her ex. She often talked about this. 'I used to go there in my ex life,' she would say and

145

I sometimes thought she meant excellent, because at other times she would say, 'That's really ex,' and this meant good. But I knew that her life had not been good and I struggled to make sense. I had a picture of the dwelling with grass growing tall and broken windows that she had showed me and I tried to put that together with the uni, which was a place she said she had once been. She would say of a place, 'I been coming here for yonks,' and I would store that carefully away for thinking about.

At the uni we always waited until someone left a table and then sat quickly down and took up their cups even if they were empty. Spoons was good at this and no matter what anyone said she always had an answer. It was warm there and sometimes we got something to eat. Or else there were rooms where she would give me a book and tell me to look at it and be still while we warmed up. It was quiet with all those books around.

On this day there was a boy trailing us though I didn't notice him, at first. Lacey. We ran against the cold. There were people who wore blankets but Spoons said she had been a blanket person and that was too grim so we just wore our clothes and made sure we didn't get too stinky. Spoons saw him and said, 'That fuckin' Lacey,' but I didn't pay any special mind. Spoons always was seeing things.

In the books room I just sat still like she told me and felt the warm slowly spreading through my legs and shoulders, though you had to make sure you didn't fall asleep. I looked at the page of the book she gave me and it was the same. It was black marks and white pages and if you stared at them for an hour you saw them start to wriggle. Sometimes Spoons would say, 'Yours any good?' She had showed me how to turn the pages in the right direction and not to go too fast or too slow. And we got warmed up.

146

Once she knew I would be able to sit there okay she showed me how to go along a hallway and wait—'If they kick you out, just come along here and stand there and if anyone asks say you're waiting for your friend.' Then she'd take me back to the books room and go off to have a wash up. On one occasion a lady said I had to go out and I stood where Spoons said and she appeared and said, 'See, I told you.'

So on this day we did that and when the lady said she was closing I saw that it must be a way of saying 'Go away', so I said thank you to her and went to stand in the right place. And this Lacey came up to me.

'She's gone,' he said.

I had never seen him before, an aging boy like me, though not as big. He had a pointed little face and dirty eyes. I saw his dirty hands, everything about him was dirty and Spoons said that if you were dirty like that they wouldn't let you be anywhere, which was true: almost right away a man said we had to go. Spoons said you should always go without saying anything, though sometimes she broke this rule. I wanted to stay but the boy Lacey said, 'She went up here,' so I went with him up into the building and away we went. 'We gotta be quick to catch her,' he said, and we went up and then down some stairs and then along a very long room with lots of people bumping into us and then outside and then back in.

I stopped. I started to go back but when I started running everyone made me stop and they made me go out, and he found me again. 'She's down there,' he said and I went with him and all the time I knew—she wasn't down there, or up here, or just through there but I had no idea how to go back. I stopped at a place where you catch a bus and sat down.

A big crowd came out of a bus, all talking, then the bus

went away and they went away, all there was was me sitting and the smell of the smoke from the pipe of the bus's engine. Then out of the smoke that Lacey. He sat down beside me and didn't say anything. I could feel how he was working this, that if he didn't say anything he would get bigger in my head and I tried to stop that but then I felt something else getting bigger which was the feeling that Spoons had gone away from me and that all there would be from now on was the city which was trying to cover everything in every direction. I held my head and looked into the hole in the air. What I could see was that Stronson had taken my Daddy from me, and Spoons had taken Henry Stroud from me, and now this Lacey was taking Spoons. Another bus came and it happened again with all the people talking and then the bus noise and the quiet with lots of blue smoke and I could see how everything went round in circles but nothing made you stay in the same place no matter how hard you rode. I remembered riding fast across the lands on my favourite horse and it seemed as though if I could only go fast enough everything would be forever. But that was before I understood that it would not be.

Lacey was thinking up something to say, I could feel it and I felt my teeth biting hard inside my head. It was going to be something horrible, it was like when the music goes up and then down before it goes bang and I could feel a steady anger getting all swole up in me. Then he opened his mouth. His teeth were little, lots of little dirty teeth all in a line and I watched them biting off the words he said, which hung in the air like the smoke and I waited for them to blow away.

He said, 'So where d'ya think she'd go?'

These words were just the words he was saying, I knew that, he was meaning something else but I couldn't think what it was and anyways it was a good idea he'd had. So I stopped thinking about that and tried to think. Immediately I had a picture but then I was afraid of giving it to Lacey as I could tell it would be different once he had it. But I had no idea.

He was waiting so very carefully.

Another bus came. My head started to pain me, it was maybe the blue smoke or maybe it was all the horrible thinking, which, because of Lacey, seemed as though there was poison in every direction. What he wanted was me and him and Spoons to be in the same place, that's what I thought, and I wanted me and Spoons and not him.

'Let's go,' he said. 'I've got something fora.' I didn't want to stop there and so I stood up but I could see he was watching me to see which way but in truth I didn't know so I started up the slope into the wind and he came alongside me. 'Where d'ya reckon?'

My mouth opened and what came out was because of my feelings which were all in a heavy lump and so my mouth said, 'I Fry burger bar.' And as I heard the words I knew that that was the end of everything and that I had done it to myself.

That Lacey didn't say anything and we just walked but I could feel him working, it was like being beside a horse that wants to bolt, you have to be making everything around you be still, but I wasn't in control and I could feel everything starting to run away from me. Then I saw something I knew and I crossed the road.

It was a big bridge. Spoons and I would come there some times and watch the cars go under and after a while it was like the pages of a book, when the black marks start to wriggle. 'Grafton Bridge,' said Lacey. 'Wrong fuckin' way. She's not on the fuckin' bridge, is she. For the I Fry ya gotta go K Road. Let's go,' he said and we went K Road. He had pointed shoes on, that made a sharp clipping noise, and there was a gap between his knees that made a hole when he walked. Vehicles were coming all the time. I had been on K Road before, I knew that. I had been on the Grafton Bridge, I had been to where the airplanes came down to land, I knew all these places, I could see pictures of them with Spoons and me there looking but I didn't know how you got from one to another; Spoons always knew that.

'Whatcha name?' he said.

Every time I told him something I could feel it going away from me but I didn't know what else to do. 'Dog,' I said.

'Dog.'

'Mr Dog,' I said.

'Who called ya Mr Dog?'

'Mr Stroud.'

'Fuck, everyone's fuckin' Mr round here. Like in fuckin' court. Who's Mr cunting Stroud?'

But I knew that if I told him then every time I thought of the comfortable room I would think of him too and so I just kept walking and tried to make the picture of the room go away. Now I knew that I didn't want that Lacey going anywhere near the I Fry Burger Bar, that if I could only get him away from it then it would stay there without him, but he was walking fast and all the time he was saying things that were going all around my head like angry fighting little birds. 'Mr Stroud must be wunna them court cunts. What kind of dog are ya? Are ya like a sausage dog or are ya a pig dog or are ya wunna them fuckin' pleece dogs? Ha ha ha. We kill them fuckin' pleece dogs. Fuckin' open their throats, man. Fuckin' let all the fucker's blood out. Anyway whatcha wanna hang with that fat-cunted old slag for? Where'd she get all that poxy face from, lookin' at that all the fuckin' time ya blind yaself. Poxy fat old slag cunt. Poxy old cunt-faced fuckin' cunt. That fuckin' cunt slag. Calls herself fuckin' Spoons. Doesn't she.'

We had come down a hill beside the vehicles all speeding and crossed between them and gone along over a little bridge which I also remembered and then I began to wonder if I might be starting to know where I was. There were dwellings here but I could see what would be around the corner, there was a big long road and then there would be the road called Jervois with the I Fry burger bar. There hadn't been anyone else walking on the footpath for a long time, just us and I saw that I could run. I knew that if I thought about this Lacey would know so I just turned around suddenly and started running back. I ran fast, as though I was after a tumbleweed—it was wonderful to just run. I heard Lacey shouting, 'Hey, wrong fuckin' way!' but I knew that, I knew where these roads went and that if I ran away carefully I would be able to hide and then when he was gone I would find my way. 'We're gonna find her,' he shouted, 'Hey! Mr Dog! Hey!' I kept running and then he shouted, 'Hey, ya fuckin' dog-brained moron, fuck ya ya fuckin' dog cunt, run ya fuckin' legs off, I don't give a fuckin' shit.'

But he was now far behind me.

Later I came back and went down under the bridge and waited.

Vehicles travelled above me and the sound was the sound that the airplanes made as they turned towards you, it made me think of the angels going across the spread of sky above the lands and all the things there that had cowered from them. It came to me then that the city knew of the lands and was connected to them; that, here under the bridge, I was connected and it was the presence of the lands inside me which gave me the hope which my Daddy said springs eternal. At some moments I had a clear picture of him, though his back was turned, and I saw that my Daddy and these pictures and the hope springing was joined by a singing thread which glowed like the trail left by a falling star, like the moon on water. I would follow this moon trail, I thought, and find Spoons; I would take her with me back to the lands.

So it was that at nightfall, when I climbed back to the road where I had made my headlong run, I strode into the gloom as though I had read the book of the city and understood its every word.

This sense that I knew what I would do carried me the length of the long road which indeed proved to lie around the corner and all through all the strides and little decisions which followed. Vehicles passed, and footpath people, each with their swishing sound, and lights pierced, and to either side doorways fell open into darkness, but I had my trail. It was a sense that the true way had been found, that I knew now which way the water would run down the mountainside and had only to follow. No one spoke to me and I have never been the one to speak first. This noisy road was a place that Spoons and I had avoided, as we were unwelcome there. But I was not on the road. I was inside a blind bubble, that goes lightly before a steady wind. I saw it clearly that Spoons was in this city and that I was in it and this meant we were in the same place and were only separated by the fact that I was not yet at the I Fry burger bar, which was there, shining white in the moonlight at the end of every picture that I could see.

Dark thoughts are like flowers which grow wrong coloured and then stand there until you kick them away. I have said I saw black roses falling, I have said I saw the dark bird flying low. Kicking such wrong-growing things does no

152

good; they must be gathered. Holding them like a black handful you must go forth and offer them. Who will take your dark flowers? Walk forth and see who will take your dark flowers.

When all I could see was pretty moonlight.

I crossed the road called Jervois, which was like a river, and came quietly along beneath the street lights hanging as though they were required to witness and to warn. How they fizzed. The sign of neon colours clicked and this made a kind of cheerful music. There on the other side of the dividing river stood the white building. I was filled with happiness. Soon I would cross the road and talk with Henry Stroud, and wait in his comfortable room until, in time, Spoons would come. Spoons and Henry would meet and so a kind of balance would be restored to the world. My happiness was giddy and I was all alive there in the night, watching. Every sound of the night came clearly, and in front of me was the white building with, inside it, the dim-lit comfortable room.

And so it was that I heard the radio song begin.

Yes, deep within that room the glowing radio was singing softly to itself. Vehicles passed before my eyes and left their swishing sounds, and in the distance there was the playing of a siren. Night dogs howled. But I heard that radio song clearly, and every word of it was like a black flower growing. To a drumbeat:

Golden days, before they end,
Whisper secrets to the wind.
Your baby won't be near you
Any more.

When the song said *wind*, then a sighing chorus of voices went eeeh-ooo, which seemed to sweep me back across the

153

lands. But, under, there was that drum that beat slow and steady, and the voice sang every word out clearly.

Tender nights, before they fly,
Send falling stars that seem to cry.
Your baby doesn't want you
Any more.

Spoons had sung this song to me in old cars. Kneeling before me, with the rain trickling down, and her eyes full of mine, she sang every word into me as though it was a lesson I had to learn.

It's over.

It was strange how suddenly everyone knew I was there. Henry Stroud came to his counter and looked out into the night, arms folded. His boy on the high chair looked also. The streetlights all leaned in. The drumbeat was like a finger tapping on a window, insistent. And that radio singer made the song come out into the night. Where was he standing, that singer, that he could see me? How did he know everything that was happening?

All the rainbows in the sky
Start to weep and say goodbye
You won't be seeing rainbows
Any more.
Setting suns, before they fall
Echo to you, 'That's all, that's all,'
But you'll see lonely sunsets,
After all.
It's over.

I knew I had done no wrong. I searched my heart for shadows. That singer was filling the night with the throbbing call of his song, which rose like a wave, higher and higher and bound to fall.

It breaks your heart in two
To know she's been untrue
But, oh, what will you do,
When she says to you
'There's someone new,
We're through,
We're through.'
It's over, it's over,
It's over.

Vehicles crossed before my eyes. The road called Jervois was a deep, swift river and there was no way to ford it. The white building glowed like a temple in a storm. From the far distance I saw a lonely figure coming slowly along the other side, with a walk that I knew. I shouted her name. I tried to feel that crazy happiness. But you can't try for happiness. It comes. It has a life of its own. It goes. I saw her and she was singing. All I could hear was that drumbeat, tapping, tapping—Spoons had her mouth open and was singing but I could hear her voice. Now from the other direction I saw him: that Lacey. He moved from one streetlight to the next, slipping from shadow to shadow.

Spoons stepped into the light of the burger bar. Henry Stroud was there watching and he saw her. She spoke to Henry, who shrugged his shoulders and spread his hands. Then there was something that made both of them turn. From the shadows a thin shape came running. His hand jerked. Then he ran on.

155

In the bright white light Spoons went down. Her hands went to her face. Her head went back and then a terrible sound came from her.

I had seen a colour in the air and then I remembered that Lacey saying, 'I got something fora.' The neon light had caught a liquid as it flew.

Nothing would stop the vehicles and so it was from a distance that I saw Henry Stroud jump over his counter and pour water into her face. The boy on my high chair handed him more water and Henry kept pouring. Spoons kept making the terrible sound. Now Lacey came running back and again I saw his hand. He struck the back of Henry Stroud, who went to his knees. Then he ran on.

I ran into the traffic. There was a horn blast, a squeal, then two vehicles crashed. I ran between.

Henry Stroud looked at me from where he was kneeling in his own blood. A knife was there in his back; blood dripped from its handle. In the white light of the burger bar he regarded me calmly. He was thinking every last thought that could be managed by his bumpy head. He was seeing what he could see. 'Chester,' he said and, though it cost him, he gave a smile to me. 'Run. Run.' I wasn't going to run but his eyes told me that it was paining him that I stayed. Then I saw that he was listening. The music was still coming from the comfortable room and Henry Stroud was catching it.

I looked for Spoons. But Spoons was gone.

Chapter Twelve

They came from time to time to pour water into me, Chowder mostly but also Lennox and once the small man Daniels. High above, vultures circled as the sun beat its way across the sky, my eyes following them until I felt there was a little whirlwind forming on my brow.

I knew that once I had had pictures inside me, names of people who had meant everything to me, but now those things were gone, replaced by a white mist in which there were wisps, no more.

They introduced me to my horse, saying her name, and putting me up on her, where my hands as I looked down on them holding the reins seemed to know what to do. I rode in the dust at the rear of the herd, looking across the backs of the cattle. My eyes squinted as though there was something up ahead that I was trying to see, but I had no idea what. All I wanted was water and I drank dry every bucket that came near me. They kept my hat wet, and my neck was always feeling the trickle of drops sliding down.

My holsters hung empty at my sides and though I knew there was something wrong with this I could not have told you what it was.

How many days passed while I was in this state is something I will never know.

Then, while we were grazing them quietly alongside a

pale canyon wall in a sunny afternoon, a change came over the cattle. I was riding last man, seeing only a landscape of haze when I heard shouting—they were shouting. They were shouting to me. 'Dog,' they shouted, 'Dog!' I tried to see.

'Dog, don't be drivin' 'em! Dog, git away! Git away! Goddammit, Dog!'

I steadied my horse and gazed about. It came to me that the cattle were moving. Now that I looked, the haze which stood everywhere before my eyes was fading to darkness, as though a swift night was falling.

There was from above a great crackle and fire reached down out of the sky. An immense *boom*! And the cattle were turning and beginning to run.

They came towards me and I had no time to move. I stood my horse. Now the cattle were like a great foaming sea, with horns flung wildly. In the sudden darkness, the tips of the horns were glowing like wildfire and every eye was rolling. The hooves thundered. My horse stood on. Now rain lashed down and my hat was torn away. I had no thoughts as to what I might do and so I stood my horse with the herd parting around me and the rain tore into my face.

That herd ran fifteen mile.

Which left me standing in the rain, hatless and drenched. The air was full of grey, and the streaking of the rain. There was nothing to be seen about, only rain, and the sudden flashes of lightning. Great puddles formed. I saw the lightning go through the water, seeking in every direction—I felt the lightning come up the legs of my horse and run like inquiring fingers over my head. I felt that. And I knew that I did. I felt my teeth in my head, my tongue in my mouth. Slowly my tongue came out and I tasted the rain. And now my ears could hear the sound of it—a drumming, like hooves, like hammers. And a splashing.

Yes, the first thing that came to me in the misty time which followed my singing beneath the wires of the pylons was a splashing sound. That was the first thing outside me that I knew. Splashing as a horse came slowly through the rain, and me there knowing the sound for what it was. Now if you work with horses you know an animal from any part. I saw white hooves stepping and sorrel legs and I knew that this was the pony we called Stubbins.

With the rain coming down on me I lifted my hands to rub my temples. I rocked in the saddle: ideas were returning to me. Stubbins, Stubbins—names and faces were flying home. Then it was my own name, Chester. I heard it and smiled— here I was, me, and knowing myself.

The name came again and now I realised that it had been spoken. The horse Stubbins was in front of me but that wasn't it. 'Chester.' I looked up and there through the heavy downpour was a woman who was speaking to me. I saw that her lips were moving and I tried to hear. Then her name came to me.

She rode Stubbins alongside my horse, who was Bess, and leaned from her saddle to peer at me. I smiled, and then saw her face light up.

'Chester,' she said again. 'This way.' She turned her horse and led me forward into the thick of the rain. My head was battered from above and my eyes ran. The horse's hooves splashed. There was water pooling inside my ears. But I was wearing a grin. Then the rain began to thin out a little and after a moment it became clear that Miss Peet was leading us south beyond the storm.

We found an overhanging rock which stood in the canyon wall and sheltered there and watched as the thick rain moved away to the north. 'They're going to be busy a couple of wet hours,' she said, and she took her sodden hat from her head, and shook it. Then she eased her bandana away. So there she was before me.

'Miss Peet,' I said and every ounce of feeling in me was in those words.

She saw that and it made her tilt her head away from me just a little; I saw her raised eyebrow. After a moment she said, 'I'm Leah—remember, Chester?'

I did remember, but too much. At the sound of her personal name I again saw the pylons and then I saw myself singing, head thrown back, guns blazing. I saw the air being burned and golden roses falling through black clouds. I looked at Leah Peet and saw her in her naked glory. This was too much for me and my hands went to my temples again.

'The pylons,' she said.

I nodded. I did not trust myself to look at her, though I wanted to. She looked away from me and I was able to compose myself. Now when I let my eyes explore she was fit to be looked upon and she saw this and looked back. She let me gaze on her face, even though it was plain that this troubled her. What a thing of loveliness she was, with the skin of her cheeks fresh-washed by the rain and, when my fingers went to it, so soft to the touch. Gently she pressed my hand away. Her eyes were lavender and green and gold and the colours in them were things that shifted, like light on troubled water. She was made so nicely that her nose and lips were fascinating to gaze upon, and so I gazed and gazed, until a big surf began to roar inside my head.

'I know I sent you there,' she said.

'No,' I protested, adamant.

'I drag trouble after me like a long chain.'

'If ever there was an angel—'

'No!' she cried and her hand came out. I saw it coming, I saw she was going to touch me and I waited. She saw too and her eyes changed, they darkened, but her hand came on and seized me by the hair and shook so that water flew. 'You're full of pylon fever,' she said.

I smiled happily. My eyes rested on the little ridge of her upper lip, where, below her nose, there was a tiny dent. A man could be cupped by that, could lie there—could lick it out with his tongue.

So she slapped me.

It was a good, firm smack and my hand went to the place. 'Chester,' she said, not without tenderness. 'The whole world is thick with fools. I don't need another fool.' She squatted now on her heels and to stay with her I had to go down also. Then we were like two men eye to eye to discuss a problem. This was how my Daddy had spoken to me, squatting on his boot heels with the dirt at hand for making pictures in. Except that we were squatting in mud. She put her hand on my shoulder and said it again, 'Chester.'

I frowned. I admit it, I was puzzled.

'All my life,' she said, 'everyone wanted what's in my trousers. Put your hand there if you have to. Go on, get it over with. I'm just like anyone. All the smoke and burnin', that's in your head. Go on, I mean it—see if I care.'

Spoons had spoken to me like this and it had similarly pained me. My eyes went down to the mud and stayed there.

Her hand was still on my shoulder and now she patted me, which was an irritation; which she had known it would be. 'Chester,' she said, 'Chester,' and it was true that there was affection in the way she used the word. So finally I looked back at her, and her loveliness broke my heart. 'Chester, they're going to come back 'fore too long. Listen to me, Chester.'

'I'm listenin',' I said.

'Tell me, Chester,' she said, 'how long have you been out here?'

'On the lands? All my life.'

'What about when you were in the city?'

She was regarding me steadily and so I returned the favour. Pictures passed now between us. I saw the I Fry burger bar with vehicles crossing continuous before it. I saw the streets of dwellings which were lined up alongside each other in every direction. I saw the city which was spreading like creeping water.

All of this she took from me. And from her? As I gazed there came to me a picture of the comfortable room. Inside her angel eyes I saw the room and was able to go freely inside it. On the floor an old carpet lay, with a pattern tiny and close worked and engaging to the eye. The walls were plain but softly glowed. On one wall a picture of trees, slim and green, through which a path ran, taking you between the trunks and into the deeps. A shaded lamp gave a soft, low light. There was a large chair with cushiony arms and a high back were your head might rest. The chair was empty, inviting—this gave me something of a chill. On the carpet now the dog Blackie looked up, tail wagging. How warm his belly would be to your bare feet.

But in that room there was the strangest thing. It stood on a side table, like a box, though a box sounds like something rude, rough and used, and this was no used thing. It was dark-polished and glowing. There were little windows in which the glow was brightest and as I stared into these windows, like yellow eyes, I saw that this was the radio, which was singing softly to itself. Closer I went and still the radio sang. Closer. But it was not my looking that mattered. I began to hear. I went into the radio and heard and what I heard was Miss Peet.

'You were there!' I said.

And this broke the spell. Now I was back in the lands, with my boots in the mud and water seeping through. Miss Peet the cowgirl was squatted with me and at our backs was the canyon wall. I saw now that the sky was clearing and, away to the north, understood that the herd had stopped running.

Miss Peet's gaze slid away.

I held my head in my hands. Waves were breaking inside me. The sky was wheeling—though, when I blinked and looked about, why, there was the steady dome of blue.

'Where are we, Chester?' she said. 'How did we come here?'

I cannot tell you how tumultuous it was to my heart to hear the need in her voice. That a creature like this was in need so deeply affected me; that there was a need I might answer. I couldn't help myself and I gazed upon her face and with every second that passed I fell and fell and kept on falling. Every song I'd ever heard was playing inside me and the knowledge of love I had been given was singing clear from every word. I loved Miss Peet and nothing could change that. I wanted to gaze upon her gorgeous face and while I was gazing to hold her.

But Miss Peet had other ideas and she would not allow this.

'Chester, Chester, make yourself crazy if you will. But listen to me.'

'Sing, Miss Peet,' I said.

She looked at me strangely and I also was surprised: where had this come from? But it was true that she had singing inside her and both of us knew that. This was a piece of truth which had come out into the drying sun and was lying there like a lizard, bright patterned and enjoying the heat on his back.

'I don't sing,' she said.

In my mind's eye I saw that radio clearly, I heard it, and I said, 'You did one time.'

'I did one time,' she agreed.

And then the lizard ran.

How, I sometimes ask myself, could it have been different? I was born to love Miss Peet and ready. My heart had been opened and something must go in. And she wanted love. Oh, she tried to deny this but when you don't want love you are dead and all the walking through the world that you can muster, all the busy days that you can line up in a row, these are no more than dogged steps taken to a horizon you know is not there. Miss Peet said she was beyond love and that all she wanted now was peace and understanding. But these are the lies we tell ourselves so that our feet can keep trudging that line. I was younger than she, though not by so many years, and had perhaps seen less, though seeing is not a matter of what has passed before your eyes but what has gone in. But I had lost everything and she, to whom everything had been given, was no judge of what she might want if only once it was denied her.

Love is the dark bird and when it is flying so strong in us we can never forget that one day it will be gone.

Miss Peet now rose and led us to the horses. 'We must ride back and help the cook,' she said. 'The boys will be tired when they come in.'

But there was no conviction in this, her voice was thick with wonder, and I knew she was moving just to be moving. I stayed where I was, stubborn, so that she was forced to come back for me. 'Chester,' she said. And I was happy to have at least provoked her to saying my name again. 'Chester, come on, cowboy.'

'Sing for me,' I said.

'Git on the pony,' she said, 'and while we ride.'

So I mounted the good horse Bess, who had stood during the rush of the cattle and saved me from going down among the churning hooves, giving her a slap of my hand to tell her that I again knew her name, and so off we rode. There were still many puddles and every crack was foaming with fresh-running water, but dry patches came like long shoals and you could smell the lands awakening to the flush of life which always springs forth after a good rain. For some time we rode companionably, just pleasured by that sensation, which is like the lift of an under-wind.

But nothing stays simple for long in this life.

Did I see a running lizard? No, but another large brown fellow was drying himself on a rock and as we passed him Miss Peet said, 'Lizard is a kind of dog, isn't he, Mr Dog. Lookit him with his tongue out.'

'Sun going right down his legs.'

'Right down his legs,' she said slowly, and looked at me as though I had made a clever remark. We were just loping along easy on the horses and then she opened her throat and everything came down.

How many times had I heard her coming like deliverance from the quiet room of Henry Stroud? She had a voice that was young and golden. But there was sadness in it, as though to be able to make such an instrument of your body took you to where the mostly earthly matters of life and death were revealed to you and then had to be held in you, a knowledge that could never be unlearned or forgotten.

165

I feel it in my legs
I feel it in my legs
It bubbles like champagne
I'm feeling it again
It's drinking me like wine
I feel it all the time
I'm feeling you.

Oh, it's filling me
It's killing me
I'm feeling you.

There were more verses, I knew, but they weren't needed. Those words, which I now understood that she, not lust-filled cowboy, had written, brought such a squeezing ache to my heart, which was learning through them that Miss Peet could not be loved, that her soul had been burned to black, and that no matter what you gave her she would only leave you on your knees out in the broken lands where the dust blew aimlessly about. Could only. Had nothing to give you, could only stare in sadness and guilt as you went the ruined way of so many.

Truly, my heart was a useless organ, attaching itself only to that which was cursed, or false, or departing.

Now she placed her gloved hand on my arm and said, as though none of this had occurred between us: 'And so tell me, Chester, what do you make of the pylons? What are they doing here? What are they doing to us?'

Well, I could hardly speak. Dragging myself up out of my well of self-pity was an agony. But the touch of her gloved fingers was insistent and so, perhaps at least in part to please her, I bent my mind. Those pylons, like great skeletons standing against the skyline—just standing, like trees, like just nothing, waiting, just waiting, for nothing . . . But everything has its purpose. Everything is doing something. That old man river, just rolling along. That steady south wind, blowing, just blowing. I stared at the pylons, growing now as I contemplated them, reaching up towards the cloudless sky, and the drooping wires between.

They were . . . busy . . .

'I reckon they're working,' I said.

'Aren't they just,' said Miss Peet.

Now that this had been stated, it was obvious. The pylons were doing something. They glowed, like forks of lightning plunged into the ground.

'But it ain't the pylons, is it,' said Miss Peet.

'No?'

'Well, do you think so?'

I shaded my eyes.

She said, 'I think it's the wires.'

Chapter Thirteen

Now, unbeknownst to me there were many kinds of dark birds which flew over these wide and dusty lands, and some of these were recording birds, seeing the world as though it was a great drama unfolding beneath them, every detail of which they held once they had seen it. If I had known of these birds. If my eyes had been able to follow. But it has been my curse, or to put it less harshly my nature, to be within the circle of what I could actually see.

Thus it was unknown to me that when Henry Stroud lay in a pool of his own blood, with the blade sticking up like a flag of conquest from his own back, that though the blood ran into the culvert and there mixed with whatever other liquids were running to the sea, some resistant, some wise part of his blood stayed within him, and so when an ambulance arrived and its medics bent over him there was in vital places, in resistant pockets, just enough of Henry the King of Dogs and Boys to keep what mattered of him alive.

This I did not know.

Everywhere that dark bird was seeing things but I was never told.

Henry's time in hospital was a period when those bumps, those declivities in his head began to make strange pictures the like of which he had not known before. They came when the light was on, colours that drifted in and out of patterns, walls of fire, vistas of eggshells. So he lay in darkness. Now the pictures were more distinct. They pained his bumps with their intensity. He rubbed his head with his thumbs. That boy with pumpkin-coloured hair, who had fallen from the boat and lost all the gear. That dog with the black mark all along his underbelly, as though he'd been crossing a swamp. Boys and dogs. Henry knew that it was always boy dogs that he liked—and boy boys. He liked poaching eggs for boys—setting them before them with a flourish. How radiant they looked, both the boys and the eggs, as though the sun had been captured. Handing out bags of salty chips, corners twisted tight. Seeing their faces as, out in the boat, with the thrown curve of ocean so infinite in every direction, tilting and peaking, their lines, with their scraps of bacon, had caught the attention of a passing fish, which was now sending a jerking of astonishment up the line into the world of sunlight. The astonishment of boys, how he loved that.

They dressed his wound and told him how lucky he was. They fed him pills in clusters, eggs from a plastic hen. He passed water for them, their eyes scarcely turned away. He accepted their drips into his arm. None of this occurred in any sense that mattered. He explored his bumps with his fingers and thought about his boys.

Behind the counter of the I Fry he slid burgers into bags and poured Cokes. But no boy was any more invited to sit on the high chair. Henry Stroud had someone in mind for that. The music, blue and gold, continued to swell softly from the comfortable room, but Henry found that, without his noticing, he had begun to favour those songs which talked of horses, or tumbleweeds, or lonesome canyons, or the tending of cattle. No love song reached him now. No dance song.

No, what he wanted was clues in the great search for the whereabouts of the boy called Mr Dog.

But Henry Stroud was not worried by the question. There had never been an unknown that had proved resistant to the often-stroked bumps and time was all that stood between them and the strange country boy called Chester Farlowe.

'Double cheese no gherkin, double chips and three cokes,' called Mr Stroud and Jervois Road gathered its paper bags and went on its way.

The girl called Spoons was living, Mr Stroud knew, on his roof, the poor disfigured thing, and every day before he left he would fill a bucket for her to pull up, and every morning he would empty her jerrycan of urine. But that was only his old-fashioned ideas about the halt and the soft headed. The girl Spoons was not, he knew, going to get him any closer to Chester.

Where would such a boy run to?

There was apparently a place were they called the wind Maria. There were places where you drifted along with the tumblin' tumbleweed. There was a man who shot Liberty Valance. But that was, Henry Stroud knew, in America,

When he applied his fingers to his bumps, what he got, repeatedly, was the Sphinx, all blown about by desert sands. Stubbed nose, eyes burned out by a million sandstorms. He studied those pictures until he found he was cursing the Sphinx for its silence and pounding his head with his shoe. He found another bump and after many of the most subtle caresses, something different began to come through. A wind, yes, which you called anything you liked, the nor'wester. That bloody door-slammer. Maria if needs be, or you could see the girl on the billboard in the field of the big ol' highway as you cruised past her. You could see something called the two-lane blacktop. You could see immense vehicles. You could see longhorns. This was the strangest thing, the way the longhorns raised a dust, into which together went the cattle, with their sounds of hooves and calling for calves and the cries of the horsemen who attended to them, and then, emerging from the dust, the great vehicles and the burning of rubber, and the mounded blacktop high with its white line that even the angels could not do without.

Mr Stroud festooned the I Fry with heavy chains and padlocks made in factories where sparks flew, and then backed his squat green vehicle out into the traffic. Spoons appeared above the parapet, her face covered as though she was devoutly observing the Muslim faith. Mr Stroud urgently motioned her down. Then, when the street was clear he tossed, with the casual expertise of a newspaper boy, a roll of bills, which Spoons caught and hid from sight.

The old green Citroën, when its accelerator was depressed, departed the scene with alacrity.

Henry Stroud headed south. This was partly because the midafternoon traffic was going that way. But there was also something that drew him. The bumps, course. They would, if he concentrated, always show which way to the golden egg—and many other things besides.

Thus he knew of Miss Peet. Not by name of course, not by any of the songs she sang. No, it was an aching at his temples. A specific bump ached for Chester. So he drove south, elbow out the window, whistling with some finesse every cowboy song he could think of.

Miss Peet and I rode up to the campfire as though we had been hard-ridin' our horses in the pursuit of the common good. It was stew and the tall-faced cook doled us a pup's portion with all the reluctance of an old king handing out diamonds to his children at inheritance time. I was confused—I knew this was an insult. Should I go for my guns? Then I remembered that my holsters were empty and I was full of shame, that I had so lost sight of my mission. But Miss Peet's holsters were full and immediately so were her hands. 'Ah, workmates,' said Boss Lennox, 'I think in general we have traditionally settled campfire matters . . .'

'By seein' who can make his mark at the furthest distance.'

'Sultation,' spoke Miss Peet in a low voice that sent the dirty dogs all looking for a darker place to bury themselves, 'if ever I see that thing again it will be shot off and lie on the ground like a booger fell out of someone's nose.'

'Chowder! Chowder!' called Lennox urgently. 'Two large plates of the best stew for these two and that is the end of the matter.' The cook did as he was asked but his slab-sided head had a trickle of sweat running down it. I knew what that trickle meant and resolved to make sure I never had my back to the cook, though that would take some doing, as the cook was like the night, which has a thousand eyes.

In the morning Boss Lennox made careful sure that Miss Peet rode west and I rode east. I was not troubled by this. Miss Peet had broken me or as near as you could get and still be walking, and I had plenty to think about. But then when I saw that low-bellied cook was coming round in a wide circle so that he and the cowgirl should meet, well, this set my blood to rising. I stood my horse and stared angrily. I was just drawing back my spurs to dig my anger into Bess when, appearing alongside me like a watchful ghost, was Boss Lennox, who reached and took my reins. I jerked angrily, but there was no point. Lennox had a good grip. I considered whether I might lash out with the end of the leash, but Lennox just held his grim little smile and waited.

'I'm just doing my job,' I protested angrily.

'Now that's a good startin' point,' said Lennox. 'You bin causing all kind of mayhem. Okay, dismount.'

'This is my horse.'

'No it ain't. It belong to the sign of the Barred S and you know it. Get down. No, not the bedroll. You had a coat. Where is that coat, exactly?'

'I got my guns,' said.

'No, sir, I don't believe you have.'

I saw how it was now—with Miss Peet, with Boss Lennox, with Spoons, with Henry Stroud. Every one of them had betrayed me and each betrayal had left me with an anger that was murderous in nature. When he asked me to step down I did so. He asked for the reins. He was just a burning outline, all hazed about with blood and vapours. His hand moved and I thought he would shoot me—I went for my holsters and found them empty. Lennox saw this and it made him laugh. But he was not a foolish man and so he did draw one gun, but casually, so as to have it ready. How I hated him up there in his leather seat, so much taller than me and all. With his free hand he was tugging at something behind his saddle. He shook it out. It was bloodstained and holed. 'Yours, I believe,' he said and tossed it, not ungently, onto the ground between us. It was my old coat, cut for a boy and fit only for rags. I left it lying there as though I was too proud to touch it, which I was. Boss Lennox cast his eyes round the red horizon, on which not a stick of shade could be seen. 'I think you'll be needin' it.'

Then he turned his horse sharply, and Bess went with him.

My Bess, whom I had trusted, who had carried me home. There she went, a horse's ass. Story of my life, studyin' forever a horse's ass.

I mastered myself, hefted the bloodstained coat and commenced to put one boot in front of the other. I was so humped up with anger I had no need of a direction. North I went, where the black birds were flying in circles, and strutting back and forth like undertakers at the foot of the pylons. When I found my guns I would shoot those birds. I would shoot everything that moved.

Lennox hollered to me. 'Don't you be goin' near them pylons now, you am already full acquainted with the consequences of that.'

'So who gives an acre of custard?'

'Son,' said Lennox, 'I know you came from the city. Now's the time for you to sit down with that coat over your brains and think. And when you done that you'll see I'm right.'

'A ranch of custard with passion fruit eyes,' I said.

But in fact I did what he suggested. Not to be doing any thinking. No, I had my direction like a compass cut into the palm of my hand. But I wanted him gone and there was no other way.

All around lay the lands, blameless and full of the only thing that can give a real teaspoon of hope to a man. Letting the red dust run through my fingers I was for a moment reminded of that other spoonful that Spoons had sung about and so many things that had been sung of came back like one of the seventh waves Mr Stroud had shown me down on the waterfront. But only for a moment. There was always the anger, coiled in the dust. When I judged Boss Lennox had lost interest in me I rose, pulled the stinking coat over my brow, and began once more to head north.

An airplane passed overhead.

I followed it with my eye. High, flashing in the sun, with lights that blipped. Also going towards the pylons. Miss Peet had said they were angels, my Daddy too, but I could not forget clinging at the airport to the hurricane wire fence and sucking in the wet, choking smell and hearing the terrible roar as the airplane had turned and aimed its blast at us—at myself and Spoons. It was as though, that day, Spoons was showing me the great acres of dime-store hinterland inside Miss Peet—the eagles that were just high-blown pieces of paper, the cactus that had green paint inside instead of sap.

But Miss Peet's world, that was where I had to live, if I was to avenge my Daddy. Spoons, it was true, had a heart, had always had more heart than anyone, but she was also just a run-around singer who liked to live in the back of old cars. I drew fingermarks in the dust. I sighed in lungfuls of red and perversely chewed them, knowing this was what would bring health to me. At my back was the mountain. I didn't have to look. I didn't have to ask how I felt about it. Despite these puny satisfactions, it was six feet of frustration which drew itself up, hardened itself against the smell of the terrible coat, then set off north, with the dirt of the red wind in my face.

The pylons as I began to approach them were all singing, like a bullet going close by. I was still a good way off when my eyes began to show me the lurid interior of things—my hand held before me, all bones. And the wires themselves still some distance away. Perhaps if I crawled I wouldn't become so dizzy? But that was no answer. As I walked, the golden roses began to fall, dead roses, bouncing once, then lying in the dust. My eyeballs could see only blistered colours, luminous, but empty, as though any meaning in them had been burned away. Now I was passing right under the wires themselves and they were talking. It made no sense. It was as though everything here—cactus, dust, the open skies, was travelling like an elongated bubble inside the drooping loops of cable. A singing of everything that lived in these lands all mixing together into a sound that both maddened and made the heart ache. Listening, I knew I would never understand. I stood, swaying. Then my mouth opened and I said, 'Mah guns.'

The dusty air cleared. Why, there they were, one half-buried right at my feet and the other far flung, but not so great a distance for boots already crusted in dirt. I began to walk. Then again my mouth opened. 'Miss Peet,' I said, and there she was. Not so far flung either: reclining on a rock, ankles crossed, hair tossed back, and, in the dead air which was her backdrop, those golden roses, burned to black at the edges of their petals, coming down through the singing darkness to bounce gently in the dust all around her. A petal landed on her but she brushed it away. She was naked of course.

She moved as though she was restless on her rock and why wasn't I coming to her?

The airplane was disappearing to the north. As I watched I heard myself say, 'Spoons.' She was in the back seat of a car—just the seat, sitting upright there in the openness of the lands. Spoons here? Spoons had her clothes on, and something like a bee-keeper's hat, which had a black veil to hide her face. I knew that if I went close she would be singing.

But instead I heard two words. I didn't speak them and afterwards I presumed they came from her. They were, 'Henry Stroud.'

I saw the final flare of the disappearing airplane. I saw Mr Stroud on his knees, dripping blood. I remembered that Lacey. Ignoring the women, each in her quarter, I set off, first towards my one gun, then the other. As I holstered each weapon, the singing from the wires increased. I was right beneath them now, on the long, red strip where nothing grew. My head was like a thousand radios and I wanted to lie down. Instead I walked. And coming to greet me, out of the haze, here was my own horse, Bess, who stood patiently while I mounted. I felt among the many pockets of the stinking coat and there were two cubes of sugar. I gave her one and sucked on the other. Immediately the radio stations increased their clamour and I heard every song I'd ever known, at once. Miss Peet was standing now. A tasselled shawl had fallen to her and she had it half about her. Her eyes begged me. Spoons watched from behind her veil. I could feel that same begging. But I turned Bess and slowly rode away.

How everything conspired to help me. And why?

Chapter Fourteen

Bess walked aimless, since her rider was no guide, but always away from the pylons. I could see the herd to the south, its dusty presence like the billow of sails in the air. I heard the distant moans of cattle and, faintly, the shouts of men. But I headed east, into the lands I had never known.

My head was still full of sickness from the pylon wires. Playing cards from some cheap whiskey bar fell about me. Strings of coloured lights, the low bustle of dogs and chickens and pigs. Everything in its wrong colour. I shook my head and had Bess plod on. I knew that if I drew a pistol and fired but once, every liquid in the place would run—eggs, whiskey bottles, bodies. But at the same time there were no walls and as I proceeded I could sense the good air filling my lungs and the lands beginning to open.

The lands to the east had always been avoided, as many mysteries were known to reside there. But Bess needed water. Soon there was a stream, but it was guarded by a water moccasin, which swayed and danced in front of Bess. I didn't want to waste a bullet on this innocent creature so I dismounted. Immediately it came towards me. Bess backed off. I did too, then found what I was looking for, a heavy rock. I crashed it down with all I had.

Beside the body of the snake, steady Bess drank her fill. So did I. I poured water on my head and felt the pylon hum begin to fade. Then we crossed.

And how different it was here. So quiet. I regarded the pylons and I began to think straight. It was as though by viewing them from this further bank you had some chance of seeing them. Just wires and standing iron—the snake had been guardian of this knowledge. But why keep you back from knowledge? Was this the boundary between the lands? So would I ever get back? But I had to go this way, if ever I were to avenge my Daddy.

The water I had drunk now hung inside me, as though it wouldn't mix. So what about Bess?

I clicked my tongue at her and so we moved off, on the far side of the river that had never been crossed. Steady Bess, who never faltered. The air was different here, and I understood that I might see anything—a signpost, a shiny vehicle from the city. I had Bess step quietly, which she didn't mind. She was pleased we had a direction. Which we did. We were riding parallel to the herd, but just a little faster than them.

And so it was that in the late afternoon we rounded a bluff, Bess and I, and saw, away and below us, the great dust lion that was Boss Lennox's operation. I dismounted and had Bess go down to her knees, for I was afraid of the cook, who pretended to love his Victrola but was really a snake's eye in a wolverine's head. Then, dismounted, Bess and I walked out of sight behind the ridge. Once I believed we had outflanked them, I climbed back aboard Bess and began to ride, hard. She was short of feed, so after a while I eased back, but now we were ahead.

A small airplane flew low over me, waggling its wings. I had never understood that they could be so small.

I felt exposed here on the eastern side of the river, as though I really was in a new land. Would my bullets fly straight here? As we pressed on I kept looking rearward, all about. Nothing.

Night was beginning to fall. How soft the air was, how

179

sweet. A man could be happy here, I thought. But there was something bothering me and I felt plagued, like a reptile too long in the sun.

We came slowly down a little draw and I began to think I might make a fire here and get some rest. As I rode out into the little opening, I saw that I was not the first to have had this thought.

A man straightened beside his horse, his arms full of firewood. 'Hello, Chester,' he said.

It was Stronson. The man who had killed my Daddy, that man who had stolen all we had. I remembered the weight of my Daddy, dragging me down. I remembered the dark bird flying. All of this took only a moment. Stronson dropped his firewood and opened his mouth to speak. Looking hard, I saw that, like me, he was a son of these lands—that he had not even once been to the city. His coat and battered hat, his weathered face, made him, like the Mexicans, like the cactus and the tumbleweed, as much a part of the landscape here as the pile of rocks with the face of Moses. There was something terribly confusing about this, something plain wrong. But it was too late for any reasoning. He had shot my Daddy and he was standing there. I shot him four times, saving the rest of my ammunition for the fights I knew were to come.

Suddenly it was over. All the years of hate. I saw that I would be different now.

There was no fire that night, no warmth. I wasn't thinking about warmth. I sat looking through the dark at Stronson's body. I couldn't go near it, though I knew I would have to. I had a righteous anger in me now, all red and roused up. I didn't have to attend to him. I didn't have to do anything, except survive my vengeance. His horse I tied to a piece of brush. Then I took myself off to a suitable distance and sat. Late in the night I hung my head and cried. I had my boy's coat on and that was about right—too short in the sleeves, narrow across the shoulders, covered in blood and dirt. This seemed a right garment for me, as though I was stuck in my past and had to wear the bloody consequences. I went back to the time before I had loosed the bullets.

My hands still shook. The guns had come into them like live things with a will of their own, my hands were just full and then the stink of gunsmoke. His body lying, curled a little around its gathered armload of firewood.

Henry Stroud drove south, caressing his temples and trying to know what could be known. He felt as though he was receiving powerful signals but he had no clue as to their nature. This didn't matter. All would be revealed. He liked the warmth of the sun on his elbow as he drove. He whistled the old songs that had once graced the air of the peaceful room, and kept his vehicle humming. Henry had once had a past of anger and violence but all that was behind him now. His wounds had healed but his strength had never returned. He liked this. It was the end of one life and the start of another.

Through the Desert Road. In Waiouru he had his tank filled and his tyres checked. Even the spare. He bought a solid reserve of sandwiches and two large bottles of Coke. The sky, now that he looked at it, was troubled to the east. He stood on the stinking forecourt for some time, taking in the sky, and the flight of birds, and most of all, the mountain.

The morning light came slowly to the eastern lands, like something grim that had to be faced. I had sat all night and was stiff. I was afraid to move. But small birds came to investigate the body and I knew there would soon be buzzards and things that went on their bellies.

But I sat while the sun rose and inside me all I could see was the black bird which goes flying to the edge of the lands, never to return. My hands, when I noticed them, were something to stare at, turning them over and over, as though they were strangers to me.

Bess shuffled her shoes.

I lifted myself and went to stand over Stronson's body. Flies were buzzin'. To one side of him was the brush he had gathered. But as I looked more closely I saw that his finger had once again written in the dust. I stared at these letters and all the world whirled about me. I saw a buzzard high and westward, just waiting, and I knew that the hard life of the lands would slowly move in and take the body as its own.

I took off my coat that was tight around my shoulders, and knelt down beside Stronson. Close now, I could see where the blood had run from his nostrils and also his mouth. It made dark pools, a little sticky. On his shirt the blood was fresher and it was there I went. Painstakingly I copied with my finger onto the back of the old coat the signs that were in the dust. Then I spread the coat in the sun to dry.

Stronson's body was heavy, so heavy. But I was older than the boy who on the mountainside had held his Daddy while he died, and so eventually I got him swung up onto the back of his horse and tied. The saddle had a holster for a rifle and this I transferred to Bess, along with the weapon itself and all the munitions that Stronson had about his person. I took his water and poured some for Bess and some also for Stronson's animal. And then we rode.

We went south. I had it in my high-flyin' eye that we were ahead of the herd, though not by more than half a day's ride.

So I urged the horses. It was not easy, they neither of them had been fed and every piece of green-looking brush we passed they paused and tore away a mouthful. I allowed this. But we could not linger. I saw another of the small airplanes, close, this time it was dropping smoke, and I knew it likely that he had seen me. The east of the river was different and I was not sure what I might encounter there.

Late in the morning there was a second vehicle in the sky. I had never seen one the shape of this before. It gave a sound that went thock, thock, thock and it moved strangely against the clouds, as though guided by impulse. I gathered the horses in the shade of an overhanging rock and we waited. When the sound was gone we moved quickly down towards the west. And there was the river.

Once again there was a guardian and I had to tie the horses. This time it was a dark, writhing fish, which broke the water and showed the in-curved teeth all down its pink throat. I didn't want to make an echoey gunshot so I searched for a large stone. But this animal was too quick for any stone. I offered it my boot and immediately it rose up and its fangs sank deep. In this way I was able to drag it away from the water. I could feel its fangs sinking through the old leather. But I was able to crush its head with the boulder and so we were free to cross. Once again the water was sweet to the mouth and both the horses and I drank our fill. Then, back on the lands again, we began north.

Was it that these two drinkings would balance inside me?

Riding, I tried to compare the nature of the regions we had been in. In our own lands, for example, the small airplane and the noisy flying machine, these things were never to be seen. The air was sweeter on the eastern bank, not as dust filled. But my own lands, home to me all my life, were where I understood the way of the world. Here, you worked. And the land supported you. And nothing, time, airplanes, nothing could ever change that. I was home and would forever now be at home. And all I had to live with was myself. I could still feel the anger and the plan I had in my head depended on it. Killing Stronson had lifted some of the savagery away from me. But there was a pool, dark as old blood, and that, I knew, had to be emptied before I could really say I was home.

We rode south, me pushing as fast as I dared.

Night fell.

Night came slowly and I knew it was now or never—this night, no other, or the cook would tune his ears, seeking like a hoot owl in the dusk, and find me. Also my horses were tired.

Stronson when my eye fell on him was not a pretty thing. Blood ran from his nose and the flies made a circus above his back. I decided I would leave him and hobbled his horse where there was good feeding. Then Bess and I rode on.

Quietly, quietly we rode and as we did I bent myself to gunfight thinking. I would be within good rifle shot, and would be behind a rock, and would be in darkness. They would all be lit by the campfire. The first must be Boss Lennox, because he would most readily figure a sensible retaliation. Then the cook because he was a survivor and he must not survive this. Henley or Daniels, it did not matter in which order, as long as they went down. Then the Kid. The Kid would be making noise enough to summon the red inside the mountain. He would charge this way and that, barking. But the greatest danger was that he would simply run from the fire and hide—wait me out. I might, at the right moment, have to call to the Kid, get his pride started. The Mexicans meanwhile would escape. I knew I never would prevent this. They would not return fire but would disappear into the dark, only to be seen when they were good and ready.

Which left Miss Peet. She would know who was at the eye-screwed end of the rifle. She might fire back. But I doubted it. No, she would sit over her dinner and await her fate.

The thought of Miss Peet made me cross-eyed with anger and confusion. She had played with me. She was the worst of them and under normal circumstances would have received the first bullet. A fistful of feeling began to swell in me and I had to calm myself. All would be resolved, as my Daddy liked to say, if everybody only let the sun roll across the sky.

Which it had nearly done. The lands were under all but complete dark now and I could see, like a stairway to the stars, the faint ladder of campfire cinders as they rose. But I needed to be closer.

I tied Bess away off to the south and went on my belly in a half circle, searching for the right position.

The old Citroën liked the long straight road south of Turangi and Henry drove as it most pleased him, one hand on his thigh, an elbow out the window—at this altitude it was cold, but he ignored that—and a single finger on the wheel. The radio sang of when old times there were not forgotten and Henry followed the song, letting it warm him as it once would have in the comfortable room.

Into the Desert Road.

There are places on that road where it bends back on itself, and dives, and goes down to where something closer to the raw heart of the planet is exposed. From the muddy banks of the Euclid-carved walls up beside him, water ran. Henry closed the window and drew his shoulders together so he was hunched over the wheel.

Nevertheless there was a pleasing aspect to steering through the curves and reverse-bends and so he drove on, in caravan with all the other cars, through Waiouru, and was soon in Taihape.

He drew to the side of the road and considered. He had gone wrong somehow. Yes. Nevertheless Taihape has its purpose and after a short pause he joined the traffic again. A mixed grill in Taihape is not a matter to be taken lightly, merely driven past. So he parked, ate a large plate of onions and offal and washed it down with three cups of grill-house coffee. A man who had run the I Fry might well make a beachhead for himself in Taihape, he reflected. But it was only a passing thought.

Sitting in his car, he closed his eyes. Immediately his bumps gave him a picture of the mountain and he knew where he was headed.

Part Four

Chapter Sixteen

And now I come to the terrible events which drowned all else that took place in that bloody year. I find it so hard to speak of them. Why bother? I am standing here on the wooden boards of my boyhood home, with my coffee, and a railing to lean on, and a beautiful golden light is spreading across the lands. I can hear the small sounds of home which mean so much to me, and my heart likes to whisper that this is rest and that by making it mine I deserve it.

But dogs never rest until the true scent is run down, and I was a dog, named so by Henry Stroud, and must run until there was no more running in me.

Thus I found a rock.

It was large enough to shelter behind and seemed almost to have been made to purpose, resembling as it did a sitting camel that Spoons had shown me once in the zoo. Not that I could fully appreciate that, then, since it was so dark, with the campfire sending long shadows out in every direction. But, a good big rock in the right place. Yes.

There they were gathered over the communal meal I had so often enjoyed and I confess that I did looking upon them feel a dull contentment inside me that almost gave me pause. But that is almost. The dull thing was nothing beside my anger, which was walking circles inside me, insistent and not to be denied.

However, it was not without regret that I settled the long barrel of Stronson's rifle in a groove in the camel's back and, taking my time, drew a bead on the chest of Boss Lennox. He was steadily eating whatever the skinny cook had produced, like the camels I saw, chewing, not talking, his senses half closed down for the night. But only half. Could I end this steadiness, this sense of patient watchfulness as it sank towards its well-earned bed? Seconds passed.

Then a dog spoke. 'Quiet,' Lennox said, so clearly that even I could hear him. But the dog gave voice again and I knew it had heard Stronson's horse, well away to my left and shuffling in its hobbles.

'There's somethin' out there!' said the Kid and he stepped through the fire and began, pistols drawn, to advance in my direction. So I shot him through the chest.

He went down without a sound. Immediately I swung back to Lennox and chest-shot him also.

Now there was an immense uproar. Henley stood and was taken. I saw the Mexicans moving, low, away towards the shelter of the herd—I let them go. Daniels was more careful, he didn't stand. With a pistol he returned fire. But he was shooting in the dark and I heard the bullets whizz harmlessly into the starry night. The rifle was a good one and, aiming carefully, I took off the top of his head.

Which left Miss Peet. She sat with her dinner and waited. She was alone now and I might have made her mine. But the anger was walking and so I shot her down.

Henry Stroud was driving slowly, north, recovering the ground he had driven before his mixed grill. At times his eyes were shut. He once again followed the twisting road down into the opened earth but he knew what he was looking for was not here. On, slowly, on, being overtaken by even the slowest vehicles, he crawled.

Once he was back in the clear air a weight lifted from him—looking up, he saw the mountain. Exactly.

On his right he saw a gravel road leading towards the distant peak. There was a wooden bar painted diagonally in orange and black, with three large padlocks and a hanging sign which swung in the local wind: 'DANGER— NO ENTRY.' But the ground was marked with tyre tracks which went around this barrier and, having checked that he wouldn't get stuck, he followed them. At first he went quickly in case someone saw him, but no one was interested and after a while he slowed and looked about. Broken lands, good only for orienteering or riding dirt bikes. The land was the colour of a dying man's face, and as stubbled and uneven. But up ahead he could see a warmer tone.

The by-road took him a couple of kilometres from the highway. It began to rise, gently at first, then more abruptly. Then, without announcement, it ended. There was an abandoned car parked across it and, to either side, other cars, all rusted and forgotten. He found a place for his own, live vehicle and came quietly to a halt. The wind rocked him. He got out, wandered about. It was plain he could drive no further.

Staring up, he saw how, before the ice cap of the mountain began, the colour of the earth was red.

His hand went to his bumps and he closed his eyes. Yes, this was what he'd been seeking. But the local wind was cold and he wrapped his arms around himself. Then he got back into the car and wound up the window. He drank from a thermos he had in the glovebox. Then, pulling a tartan blanket over from the back seat, he stretched out as best he could and went to sleep.

I was aware that the Mexicans might try to circle round behind me and I shifted as quietly as I could behind the camel-shaped rock so as to improve my position. But there was no need. The night was utterly silent and inside I knew that it would stay that way. So silent. As though the silence was close over you, seeking for any sound it might capture. I could not afford to sob.

But sobs rose in me. The anger was gone. What was I without that anger? A pathetic thing, that had nothing to call on. Around me the silence of the lands was not a reproach. It was a question.

With the dawn I rose stiffly from my secure place behind the camel and began to look about. The whole story could plainly be seen. I reloaded the rifle, checked that my pistols were read to be drawn, and ventured forth. It might be that the Mexicans would shoot and if they did they would not miss. But I no longer had the anger to force me to address this. I was now a creature of fate.

I went to the Kid first. His body was twisted so that his face ploughed into the dirt. He had fallen hard. A red strain had spread across his back and this the flies were clouded over, each fighting for ownership of a thing that would never fight back.

The Kid was an island, the mainland was ahead. Yet I lingered there, afraid. I studied how he had fallen, how his body had taken its mortal blow.

But then a voice was to be heard.

I ran in terror but there was nowhere to run. A voice, dry, ruined, had come from the campfire.

'Chester.'

So, rifle at the ready, I went. There was Boss Lennox, thrown backwards, mouth open, eyes too, and in them the dark bird. There were Daniels and Henley, each of then turned away as though to seek privacy in death. And there, lying to one side, shirt stained with the particular dull red that was entering me to take up permanent residence among the colours that lived inside, was Miss Peet. 'Chester,' said the voice and now I could hear its pain, 'come down here.'

Could I disobey? Yes, there was an impulse that flared briefly: kill her now. But there was no anger in this and so it had no meaning. Down I went, to my knees.

Her face was streaked in blood. There was blood on her shirt-waist, and on her belly, and on her chaps. I began to daub at this blood on her face, but she said, 'No.' Her voice was so terrible and low that it must be obeyed. So I knelt in the dirt, my boots in the last of the embers, and made myself look into her eyes. 'I have kept myself alive all night,' she said, 'that you might hear me. Will you hear me, Chester?'

What answer is possible? I nodded my sorry head. Tears were already streaming from my eyes. 'Will you hear my confession?' she asked.

I knew nothing of the church. But it was not church she wanted. 'Chester,' said the terrible voice and each word it spoke taught me what I had done. 'Chester, I never did what was wrong. But I did wrong—how can that be? All I did was sing, Chester, and around me the world destroyed itself. Men came, Chester, and broke themselves. I did nothing. And yet this cannot have been—can it? Don't cry, Chester, it's no use to me. I have hung on all night and now you must hear me.'

My hand moved to make her more comfortable but that voice with all of life and death in it said, 'No.'

'I must be bad, Chester, because everywhere I go bad occurs. It's my face, I would say, it's my voice, my body, and these were not things that I had made. But they were me. Chester? They were me.'

I could not follow these words but they were making her

193

suffer. 'Miss Peet,' I said. Her eyes lifted themselves to mine. But all I had to say was her name, which I said over and over, my face in my hands.

'I confess, Chester,' she said. 'Do you hear?'

I could hear from her voice that she was fading. A thought came to me. Yes, even at that time, in the bloody dawn, I had a thought for myself and so I unrolled my boy's coat and asked, 'What do these letters say?'

Reading them was her final punishment. She was very slow. But the words came out. 'It says, "Chester, I am your father."'

Then her head fell and I saw her face in the dirt. 'Miss Peet!' I cried.

She tried to say it again: 'Do you hear my confession, Chester?' Her lips were in the dirt and the words made dirt come into her mouth. Again she said these words and this time it was more painful to her.

So, not understanding what I was doing, I spoke. I said, 'I do hear, Leah.' Then when I poured water into her mouth she did not stir and the water ran away into the red dirt, leaving an ugly darkness.

Henry Stroud had a swig of Coke, followed with the last of the coffee from his thermos, then stepped outside to answer the call of nature. As he darkened the soil, he scanned around, but he was not really looking. He had already seen everything he needed to see. It was cold. He zipped his jacket, tucked his trousers into his socks. The tartan blanket he drew across his shoulders.

As he climbed he whistled. This was too hard and soon there was only a silent exhalation coming from his lips. The music had started in his head though. The old songs, with so much space and sky in them—where the deer and the antelope play. He wished he had a dog with him, or a boy. Well, that was what this was all about, wasn't it.

His wound meant that he moved slowly. His strength was gone and he knew he would never again threaten anyone. This was a loss he took personally, it was the loss of part of the idea of himself. He could not quite straighten properly. Your life changes in an instant, you crossed a bridge without seeing what was down in the water and then could never go back.

But this did not mean that strange things could not happen in life and that you could not enjoy them. This air, for instance. He was gasping. But he did not need to look around to know that he was walking himself to a different place.

I dug no graves. Even Miss Peet I left lying where the animals and birds would find her. I found a nosebag for Bess and for Stronson's horse, mounted, and began to ride south.

Stronson's horse. Stronson. Oh, Stronson. Miss Peet's reading to me had opened a hole in my head and now pictures were coming to me. Stronson leaving a message in the dust when he'd discovered my campfire. The narrow-headed cook's harsh words about him. Stronson on the mountainside, his heels crunching away as I held my Daddy's body in my boy's arms. Expressions on faces; glances and pauses, they all came to me and I saw each one as though it had a new message of fear for me. If Stronson was my father, who was my Daddy, who had sung to me, and given me all my knowledge, and made me understand that I was loved?

Meanwhile the lands unfolded. Bess had never been a horse of ours but surely she knew the way south and was carrying me, and my pictures, towards some destination she was familiar with. I let her have her head. Stronson's horse followed on the long rope, which tugged from time to time—he was not so happy with this way. The clouds moved slowly overhead, keeping pace with us. I saw signs in the dust, little markings where birds or belly-runners had made their way. High, vultures and buzzards were making their way south also. I gave them no mind. I felt light in the head. Despite the pictures, which would not stop coming, I felt the beloved air of home coming into me and making me whole. There was room. The anger was gone and it left such a space as might house an entire pasturelands complete with cattlebeasts and riders.

So I was carried, south, and then, without my first noticing, up. Yes, gradually I was going up, and when I realised this I put the spurs to Bess and had us hurry. But this was not right and soon we slowed. I could not make myself look ahead. But up, up, we climbed.

Henry for his part was climbing much more slowly. But he was making progress—when he looked back his car was very small, hardly to be distinguished.

And then when he looked up there was a cabin.

He stood, resting. Without raising the dust, he moved sideways until he had found a cactus to be in the shadow of. He sat and watched.

It was a low, wooden cabin, built into the mountainside, with perhaps several small rooms at the back and then, he guessed, a large room which was what you stepped into when you came inside. A chimney rose from this large room. Then, across the front of the structure, there was a long wooden veranda, with a rail for tying horses and for leaning on while you looked out over the lands. Henry turned and looked to see what you might see from this veranda. The whole of what he would call a ranch. The view went on forever. In the far north he could see a line of pylons. Closer, there was a low cloud of dust and Henry stared at this for some time before he understood it was a herd of cattle. Then, down to his right, he saw a horseman slowly ascending the mountainside towards him.

The door of the cabin was open and as he glanced up he saw a bird fly out of it. So, no one in the cabin. Snakes, probably, thought Henry—and then a surge of strangeness came over him, his bumps sang. Horses, cattle, fine, but snakes, here in New Zealand?

Though he had known it would be so.

He wished he had a gun. But what use was a gun to him, really? So he picked himself up, and made the last small climb to the cabin. It was silent. But various signs suggested that someone had been living here recently. Henry looked keenly about, reading whatever there was to be read. Then he sat himself down on the edge of the veranda and waited.

Now I looked up and saw the cabin. I had been expecting a ruin—it was many years since my Daddy and I had made our home here. But it was clearly alive, lived in. Worst of all, someone was there.

I stood Bess and studied. The was no point in running, we were seen already. A man was on the boards out front— sitting. Gazing at me. I thought of my guns. But my anger had been left at the campfire and anyway this man was grinning at me. Not a grin of triumph, or possession. No, it was a grin of knowledge. This man knew me.

I was looking up, and the sun, curling around the edge of the mountain, was in my eyes. But then he waved a hand and I saw.

197

Chapter Seventeen

Slowly I rode Bess up the mountainside until I was at the railing. I tied her. I climbed down and stood in the red dirt of our home. I took off my hat. 'Mr Stroud,' I said.

'Mr Dog,' said Henry.

As I crossed the last few steps to the cabin, he stood so as to make room for me, and I saw that he was bent, just a little, from where Lacey's knife had entered him. Feelings came and went inside me like hard-working birds—flying urgently.

We stood side by side at the rail, looking out over the lands. How beautiful they looked in the late sun. But they were changed. The black highway was no longer just the black highway. The iron rails that the trains ran on no longer seemed small, long pieces of metal. The pylons, on the far horizon, were humming, you could hear it easy. I was filled with a terrible sadness. And where was my Daddy? Gone, gone, never to return. I was strongly gripped by these feelings and my eyes swam. Then beside me a voice spoke. It said, 'Burger time, Mr Dog.'

Mr Stroud and I explored the cabin. Yes, it had been lived in and recently. Suddenly I knew who and I said out loud, 'Stronson.'

Everything was wrong and I felt the tears running down my cheeks. Mr Stroud spoke again. 'I need wood for the cooker, Mr Dog.' And so, grateful for the task, I went to collect wood.

We ate on the boards out front that Mr Stroud called the veranda. It was strange having him there, his city eyes seeing everything. But food, served when you're hungry, makes everything belong to the same world. He had made something from strips of jerky and potatoes and beans, which we washed down with coffee. The coffee brought tears to my eyes and soon I was sobbing as though I had something inside me that had to come out. I was ashamed to weep like this in front of him but he sat beside me so comfortable and solid and when I had stopped rocking back and forth he said, 'Alright now, Mr Dog?'

I got the words out. 'Alright, Mr Stroud.'

He brought us more coffee and then without warning I began to talk. It was late in the afternoon, the clouds were lifting away, and many miles could be seen of the red lands. This was where my misdeeds had been done. I started with my Daddy shot down by the coward Stronson on the mountaintop. I described my journey to the city, and my return. I showed him my boy's coat with the words of blood on it. I described killing them all.

It was as though to tell it placed these deeds in the lands, brought them here never to be erased. To tell it stained that place, changed it, which had always been my home, and not for the first time I felt I was killing the thing I loved. But on I talked, on and on.

Mr Stroud made more coffee.

Then he said, 'Well, that is quite a big story you have there, Mr Dog, and I can see why a man might cry over it.' This was the first time ever he had called me a man. 'Now I'll tell you what we'll do. We'll look this cabin over and see where we will spend the night. We'll put all of the things you say belonged to Stronson out here on one end of the veranda and we'll keep all the things that belonged to you and your

Daddy. Come on now, Mr Dog, dark soon.'

'But what . . .'

'In the morning, Chester,' he said, and he motioned me with his hand to go inside.

So we started. My room, which was dark in the mornings but saw the sun go down, we did last. Mr Stroud had a very clear idea of what was to be done and I just followed, taking orders. This was such a pleasure. Stronson had slept in the other room, which had been my Daddy's, and as we made it bare and clean Mr Stroud said, 'I'll be sleeping in here.'

When I woke in the morning I could smell the coffee, just as my Daddy had done it, and I confess that yet again I had a little weep. But Mr Stroud roused me and soon we were back on the veranda, a little chilly in the morning air, but such a sweet place to be. He brought me breakfast on a plate, he served me. I noticed again that his movements were especially careful, hesitant even, he who had always moved like destiny, and I thought of the terrible events which had taken place on the footpath outside the I Fry. When I was done he sat down beside me, both of us with coffee, and he looked out as far as he could see. His hand came up to caress the bumps on his head and I watched and listened and waited. Finally he said, 'You will never know who was your father and who was your Daddy, Chester. That knowledge has sunk into the dirt of this place and can never be dug up. The bodies of those you killed, they will sink also. The Mexicans will run the herd and they will do with it what they choose. They may drive it to some railhead and sell it. They may recruit more Mexicans and run it here on what you call the lands. They may even come to you and say, 'Boss Chester, what are you wanting to do?'

I nodded, trying to take this in.

I could feel a hole opening in me. Never to know, never to understand.

Then he said, 'I'm going to stay here, Mr Dog—that okay with you?'

I tipped out the last of my coffee and watched it sink into the dirt. I looked sideways at him. Mr Stroud, who had saved me, and here now he always would be. My head went down and I began to weep again.

Again, his fingers in my hair. The comfortableness of him. He said, 'I take it that's a yes, Mr Dog.' And I nodded.

All day we cleaned that cabin and tidied it. I heard myself whistling. I had a hole where my Daddy resided, yes, but in that hole—and I knew it was disloyal to see this, but I did see it—was Mr Stroud.

We were cleaning the wood stove, the way we had cleaned the hotplate at the I Fry, when Mr Stroud said quietly, 'Notice anything?'

It annoyed me that I couldn't answer.

He led me outside. We stood looking at Stronson's things. I didn't see anything, but Mr Stroud was staring at them so I looked harder.

They were fading.

Chapter Eighteen

In the middle of the afternoon he said, 'Mr Dog, I'm getting thin on that jerky. I believe you best go shoot us something for dinner.'

So proud I was when I rode off on Bess. He wasn't to be seen, no wave from the veranda, but I knew he was in the cabin—in the hole inside me—and that made me so happy. I came back with three jackrabbits and he took them possessively. No words, but I knew I had done well.

And so we ate on the veranda boards again. Stronson's things could still be seen, especially when you weren't thinking and they caught the corner of your eye. But, looked at straight, they were like a dust cloud, that would soon settle, leaving no trace in the air.

Late, when we were in our separate rooms, I heard a wolf howl. Then an answer. I thought of the Mexicans, just two of them, and a dog, patrolling. I could see the blue-faced moon, marking the ridges of the backs of the cattle. The smell of the wind from the south came and it was so fresh and full of promise. I pulled my blanket up to my shoulder, and was soon where no wolves could ever reach me.

Next morning, once we had breakfasted, Mr Stroud said, 'I have something to show you, Chester.' He took me into my Daddy's room, which was now his room, and, taking a breath because of his wound, bent low, to the bottom drawer of the old Scotch chest which had always stood there. He struggled with the drawer, but would not let me help him. I saw cloth—clothes. He drew out an article of clothing. It was made for a woman—a dress, tight-waisted and full, in dark green. In places it was faded. Lovingly he laid it on the bed that had been my Daddy's.

There were five dresses, each one carefully folded—the creases were old. Then he drew from the bottom of the drawer a framed picture. It was a silhouette, completely black, laid upon a base of white, as might be cut at a fair. I held it and stared at it. I could see the outline of a woman's face, the curls of her hair, but no more. 'I think these now will reside in your room,' he said.

So I took them and laid them tenderly on my bed.

Then we returned to the veranda. I was full of whirling thoughts and he brought me coffee and let me be. It was strange to be idle here, my Daddy had kept us working. We sat only at the day's end, when the sun was cutting the lands into long shapes that revealed the souls and hearts of everything. But now I could tell was a time for contemplation, when thought was what there was to do. I could hear Mr Stroud at work tidying the kitchen, and it was a sound that made me happy.

When he joined me he sat down slowly and then asked, 'So what comes to mind, Chester?'

I said, 'The pylons. The pylons and Miss Peet and what was the connection?'

'Yes. I've been thinking on that. I think it's like this. The pylons want something—is that true?

'The wires,' I said.

'Yes, the wires. The wires want to take all that is here. They want to wire it to the city.'

'Miss Peet?'

'Especially Miss Peet. I think she was a singer. I can remember some of the songs she sang, that came out of my radio. Miss Leah Peet, is that right?' But it wasn't a question. He knew. He had put his fingers to his bumps and remembered and thought. It was a head that kept all that entered it.

'They want to take all that is here?'

'That's my understanding,' he said.

'And when they've taken it?'

'It's gone.' He gazed into the dusty distance and it was as though he was saying goodbye to it. I was filled with a sense of horror. 'You don't need to worry,' he said. 'If the pylons were any good, they would have taken all this years ago. It's a crude system,' he said. 'But it's there and we've gotta respect it.'

I liked hearing him say 'we'.

'I wouldn't go visiting near the pylons,' he said, 'not if I were you. I think you had a lucky escape, there.'

I thought of Miss Peet, eaten by the pylons, by the wires. But this was not true. Miss Peet was lost because of a bullet from my rifle.

I shot us a turkey and he sat on the veranda and pulled its feathers. They blew away across the mountainside, spreading like a cape. Once a turkey gobbling and now this. If I wished, I could see death and endings and loss everywhere I looked. But Mr Stroud was cheerful. I could hear him whistling under his breath, the song about the wind being called Maria. He tossed the bird this way and that. All the insides, which my Daddy and I threw away, he kept, and I knew he would cook them. He was content and I wished I could be like that.

High, never moving in the late afternoon sun, an eagle

passed, spread wings tilting occasionally, and all the lands, which had been here forever, seemed, under that eagle's eye, to be a thing which could never pass.

I said, 'I want Spoons to come here.'

'Ah-ha,' said Henry Stroud. He took this information into himself, measuring its meaning. 'Anything else, Mr Dog?' I shook my head. 'Well,' he said, 'it might be. I don't see any reason against. Yep, I can see that. And I,' he went on, 'I think I want my radio. Do you mind if I bring my radio?'

'And the carpet,' I said, 'and the beautiful low light.'

Now an old song could be heard:

When the cowboys
Are all sleeping
And the fire burns low
And the herd has decided
It has no place to go
When the horses are settled
And the wind's died right down
And the dust has returned
To its place on the ground
That's when my old feet
Can rest and be still
All day I've spent running
From gully to hill.

   My dreams full of chasing
   And doing my part
   I'm a dog for the cowboys
   And that fills my heart
   Yes I'm a dog for the cowboys
   And my feet print the dust
   In this old world of sorrows

That is enough
Yes I'm a dog for the cowboys
And that is enough.

Henry and Chester nodding together there on the veranda.

Now Henry said, 'I'll sleep in the big room here,' indicating behind him. There was a wince, but only from his wound. 'I will take one end and make a bed along there and the rest of the room will be for my radio and so forth. And Lady Spoons will have the room I am in now.' I considered this. It was not what I had thought. But I saw that he was right. Yes, that was the way to do it. 'And the two of you will have horses and will go riding out for what we need. I won't be riding, not again. But you two can ride out and I can watch over you.'

Then he laid the bird aside and his voice darkened. 'You know, Chester, that things can go from here.' His glance led my eyes to the end of the veranda, where Stronson's possessions were no longer to be seen. 'And in the same way, I think that things can come.'

I thought this over. His voice was full of waning. 'What things?' I said.

'I don't know,' he said. 'This place gives rise to and it dispenses with. Your rifle moved every piece on the chessboard, I think.'

Far out, travelling slowly south, the dust of the herd could be seen as it made its way into the distance. 'What things?' I said, maybe a little stubbornly.

His hand went to his bumps. 'Riders,' he said. And he took up the bird and took it inside.

Far below on the blacktop of the highway I could see his green car as he made his way north. Did he wave out the window? I couldn't see, and my eye let him go. But my gaze stayed on the distance. There were the pylons, a good bird's flight away, but there, and my eyes seemed to make out the wires, just swaying slightly, as though active. Then the shapes of the lands, so familiar to me, with the folds and deep cuttings, as though mighty rivers had once flowed here. And the colours, so familiar. Above, the clouds, arranged in layers, and their shadows moving slowly over the lands below.

Behind me was the mountain, with my Daddy inside it, and who knew what else? Perhaps all that I knew had come from inside it, and one day might return. Well, in time. What I was in fact listening for was the music. I could sense that it was there, in the comfortable room behind me. The many-patterned carpet had been laid, and the low lamp was burning. Spoons was in her room, dressing or undressing, getting ready for a bath, singing along when the radio played Roy Orbison. Henry was at the stove and calling for more wood. Standing on the veranda now, I had a hot cup of coffee in my hands, which I drank slowly so as not to be scalded. When it was done, I again tipped the last dark drops into the dirt and again watched them fade. My eyes went round the horizon for the last time, then I turned inside.

No riders.